Murder Being Once Done

RUTH RENDELL

Murder Being Once Done

BOOK CLUB ASSOCIATES
LONDON

This edition published 1972 by
Book Club Associates
by arrangement with Hutchinson Publishing Group Ltd.

Printed in Great Britain
by The Anchor Press Ltd.,
and bound by Wm. Brendon & Son Ltd.,
both of Tiptree, Essex

For Frits and Nelly Twiss

The chapter heading quotations are taken from
Sir Thomas More's *Utopia* in the Ralph Robinson
translation of 1551

1

*The sick . . . they see to with great affection, and let
nothing at all pass concerning either physic or good
diet whereby they may be restored to their health.*

WHEN Wexford came downstairs in the morning his nephew
had already left for work and the women, with the
fiendish gusto of amateur dieticians, were preparing a con-
valescent's breakfast. It had been like that every day since he
arrived in London. They kept him in bed till ten; they ran
his bath for him; one of them waited for him at the foot of
the stairs, holding out a hand in case he fell, a lunatic smile
of encouragement on her face.

The other—this morning it was his nephew's wife, Denise—
presided over the meagre spread on the dining-room table.
Wexford viewed it grimly: two circular biscuits apparently
composed of sawdust and glue, a pat of unsaturated fat, half a
sugarless grapefruit, black coffee and, crowning horror, a glass
of wobbly pallid substance he took to be yoghurt. His own
wife, trotting behind him from her post as staircase attendant,
proffered two white pills and a glass of water.

'This diet,' he said, 'is going to be the death of me.'

'Oh, it's not so bad. Imagine if you were diabetic as well.'

'Who,' quoted Wexford, 'can hold a fire in his hand by
thinking on the frosty Caucasus?'

He swallowed the pills and, having shown his contempt for
the yoghurt by covering it with his napkin, began to eat sour
grapefruit under their solicitous eyes.

7

'Where are you going for your walk this morning, Uncle Reg?'

He had been to look at Carlyle's house; he had explored the King's Road, eyeing with equal amazement the shops and the people who shopped in them; he had stood at the entrance to Stamford Bridge football ground and actually seen Alan Hudson; he had traversed every exquisite little Chelsea square, admired the grandeur of The Boltons and the quaint corners of Walham Green; on aching feet he had tramped through the Chenil Galleries and the antique market. They liked him to walk. In the afternoons they encouraged him to go with them in taxis and tube trains to the Natural History Museum and Brompton Oratory and Harrods. As long as he didn't think too much or tax his brain by asking a lot of questions, or stay up late or try to go into pubs, they jollied him along with a kind of humouring indulgence.

'Where am I going this morning?' he said. 'Maybe down to the Embankment.'

'Oh, yes, do. What a good idea!'

'I thought I'd have a look at that statue.'

'St Thomas More,' said Denise, who was a Catholic.

'Sir Thomas,' said Wexford, who wasn't.

'St Thomas, Uncle Reg.' Denise whisked away the unsaturated fat before Wexford could eat too much of it. 'And this afternoon, if it isn't too cold, we'll all go and look at Peter Pan in Kensington Gardens.'

But it was cold, bitingly cold and rather foggy. He was glad of the scarf his wife had wrapped round his neck, although he would have preferred her not to have gazed so piteously into his eyes while doing so, as if she feared the next time she saw him he would be on a mortuary slab. He didn't feel ill, only bored. There weren't even very many people about this morning to divert him with their flowing hair, beads, medieval ironmongery, flower-painted boots and shaggy coats matching shaggy Afghan hounds. The teeming young, who usually drifted past him incuriously, were this morning congregated in the little cafés with names like Friendly Frodo and The Love Conception.

Theresa Street, where his nephew's house was, lay on the borders of fashionable Chelsea, outside them if you hold that the King's Road ends at Beaufort Street. Wexford was beginning to pick up these bits of with-it lore. He had to have something to keep his mind going. He crossed the King's Road by the World's End and made his way towards the river.

It was lead-coloured this morning, the 29th of February. Fog robbed the Embankment of colour and even the Albert Bridge, whose blue and white slenderness he liked, had lost its Wedgwood look and loomed out of the mist as a sepia skeleton. He walked down the bridge and then back and across the road, blinking his eye and rubbing it. There was nothing in his eye but the small blind spot, no immovable grain of dust. It only felt that way and always would now, he supposed.

The seated statue which confronted him returned his gaze with darkling kindliness. It seemed preoccupied with affairs of state, affairs of grace and matters utopian. What with his eye and the fog, he had to approach more closely to be sure that it was, in fact, a coloured statue, not naked bronze or stone, but tinted black and gold.

He had never seen it before, but he had, of course, seen pictures of the philosopher, statesman and martyr, notably the Holbein drawing of Sir Thomas and his family. Until now, however, the close resemblance of the reproduced face to a known and living face had not struck him. Only replace that saintly gravity with an impish gleam, he thought, those mild resigned lips with the curve of irony, and it was Dr Crocker to the life.

Feeling like Ahab in Naboth's vineyard, Wexford addressed the statue aloud.

'Hast thou found me, O mine enemy?'

Sir Thomas continued to reflect on an ideal state or perhaps on the perils of Reformation. His face, possibly by a trick of the drifting mist, seemed to have grown even more grave, not to say comminatory. Now it wore precisely the expression Crocker's had worn that Sunday in Kingsmarkham when he had diagnosed a thrombosis in his friend's eye.

'God knows, Reg, I warned you often enough. I told you to lose weight, I told you to take things easier, and how many times have I told you to stay off the booze?'

'All right. What now? Will I have another?'

'If you do, it may be your brain the clot touches, not your eye. You'd better get away somewhere for a complete rest. I suggest a month away.'

'I can't go away for a month!'

'Why not? Nobody's indispensable.'

'Oh, yes, they are. What about Winston Churchill? What about Nelson?'

'The trouble with you, apart from high blood pressure, is delusions of grandeur. Take Dora away to the seaside.'

'In *February*? Anyway, I hate the sea. And I can't go away to the country. I live in the country.'

The doctor took his sphygmomanometer out of his bag and, silently rolling up Wexford's sleeve, bound the instrument to his arm. 'Perhaps the best thing,' said Crocker, without revealing his findings, 'will be to send you to my brother's health farm in Norfolk.'

'God! What would I do with myself all day?'

'By the time,' said Crocker dreamily, 'you've had nothing but orange juice and sauna baths for three days you won't have the strength to do anything. The last patient I sent there was too weak to lift the phone and call his wife. He'd only been married a month and he was very much in love.'

Wexford gave the doctor a lowering cowed glance. 'May God protect me from my friends. I'll tell you what, I'll go to London. How would that do? My nephew's always asking us. You know the one I mean, my sister's boy, Howard, the superintendent with the Met. He's got a house in Chelsea.'

'All right. But no late nights, Reg. No participation in

swinging London. No alcohol. I'm giving you a diet sheet one thousand calories a day. It sounds a lot, but, believe me, it ain't.'

'It's starvation,' said Wexford to the statue.

He had started to shiver, standing there and brooding. Time to get back for the pre-lunch rest and glass of tomato juice they made him have. One thing, he wasn't joining any Peter Pan expedition afterwards. He didn't believe in fairies and one statue a day was enough. A bus ride, maybe. But not on that one he could see trundling up Cremorne Road and ultimately bound for Kenbourne Vale. Howard had made it quite plain in his negative gracious way that that was one district of London in which his uncle wouldn't be welcome.

'And don't get any ideas about talking shop with that nephew of yours,' had been Crocker's parting words. 'You've got to get away from all that for a bit. Where did you say his manor is, Kenbourne Vale?'

Wexford nodded. 'Tough sort of place, I'm told.'

'They don't come any tougher. I trained there at St Biddulph's.' As always when speaking to the green rustic of his years in the metropolis, Crocker wore his Mr Worldly Wiseman expression and his voice became gently patronising. 'There's an enormous cemetery, bigger than Kensal Green and more bizarre than Brompton, with vast tombs and a few minor royals buried there, and the geriatric wards of the hospital overlook the cemetery just to show the poor old things what their next stop'll be. Apart from that, the place is miles of mouldering terraces containing two classes of persons: *Threepenny Opera* crooks and the undeserving poor.'

'I daresay,' said Wexford, getting his own back, 'it's changed in the intervening thirty years.'

'Nothing to interest you, anyway,' the doctor snapped. 'I don't want you poking your nose into Kenbourne Vale's crime, so you can turn a deaf ear to your nephew's invitations.'

Invitations! Wexford laughed bitterly to himself. Much chance he had of turning a deaf ear when Howard, in the ten

11

days since his uncle's arrival, hadn't spoken a single word even to indicate that he was a policeman, let alone suggested a visit to the Yard or an introduction to his inspector. Not that he was neglectful. Howard was courtesy itself, the most considerate of hosts, and, when it came to conversation, quite deferential in matters, for instance, of literature, in spite of his Cambridge First. Only on the subject nearest to his uncle's heart (and, presumably, to his own) was he discouragingly silent.

It was obvious why. Detective superintendents, holding high office in a London crime squad, are above talking shop with detective chief inspectors from Sussex. Men who have inherited houses in Chelsea will not condescend very far with men who occupy three-bedroom villas in the provinces. It was the way of the world.

Howard was a snob. A kind, attentive thoughtful snob, but a snob just the same. And that was why, that above all, Wexford wished he had gone to the seaside or the health farm. As he turned into Theresa Street he wondered if he could stand another evening in Denise's elegant drawing room, the women chatting clothes and cooking, while he and Howard exchanged small talk on the weather and the sights of London, interspersed with bits of Eliot.

'You must try and see some City churches while you're here.'

'St Magnus Martyr, white and gold?'

'St Mary Woolnoth, who tolls the hours with a dead sound on the final stroke of nine!'

Nearly another fortnight of it.

They wouldn't go to Peter Pan without him. Some other day, they said, resigning themselves without too much anguish to attending Harvey Nichols' fashion show instead. He swallowed his pills, ate his poached fish and fruit salad, and watched them leave the house, each suitably attired as befitted thirty years and fifty-five, Denise in purple velvet, feathers and a picture hat, Dora in the ranch mink he had bought her for their silver wedding. They got on fine, those two. As well as their joint determination to treat him like a retarded six-year-old with a congenital disease, they seemed to have every female taste in common.

Everybody got on fine but him: Crocker with his twenty-eight-inch waistline; Mike Burden in Kingsmarkham police station getting the feel of his, Wexford's, mantle on his shoulders and liking it; Howard departing every day for his secret hush-hush job which might have been in Whitehall rather than Kenbourne Vale nick, for all he told his uncle to the contrary.

Self-pity never got anyone anywhere. He mustn't look on it as a holiday but as a rest cure. It was time to forget all those pleasant visions he had had in the train to Victoria, the pictures of himself helping Howard with his enquiries, even giving—he blushed to recall it—a few little words of advice. Crocker had been right. He did have delusions of grandeur.

They had been knocked on the head here all right. The house itself was enough to cut any provincial down to size. It wasn't a big house, but then, nor is the Taj Mahal very big. What worried him and made him tread like a cat burglar were the exquisite appointments of the place: the fragile furniture, the pieces of Chinese porcelain balanced on tiny tables, the screens he was always nearly knocking over, Denise's flower arrangements. Weird, exotic, heterogeneous, they troubled him as almost daily a fresh confection appeared. He could never be sure whether a rosebud was intended to lie in that negligent fashion on the marble surface of a table or whether it had been inadvertently dislodged from its fellows in the majolica bowl by his own clumsy hand.

The temperature of the house, as he put it to himself, exaggerating slightly, was that of a Greek beach at noon in August. If you had the figure for it you could have gone about quite happily in a bikini. He wondered why Denise, who had, didn't. And how did the flowers survive, the daffodils ill-at-ease among avocado-pear plants?

When he had had his hour's rest with his feet up he took

the two library tickets Denise had left him and walked down to Manresa Road. Anything to get out of that house. The beautiful, warm, dull silence of it depressed him.

Why shouldn't he go home?

Dora could stay on if she liked. He thought of home with an ache in his belly that was only partly due to hunger. Home. The green Sussex meadows, the pine forest, the High Street full of people he knew and who knew him, the police station and Mike glad to see him back; his own house, cold as an English house should be except in front of the one great roaring fire; proper food and proper bread and in the fridge the secret beer cans.

Might as well get out a couple of books, though. Something to read in the train, and he could send them back to Denise by post. He chose a novel, and then, because he now felt he knew the old boy and had actually had a sort of conversation with him, More's *Utopia*. After that he had nothing at all to do so he sat down for a long while in the library, not even opening the books but thinking about home.

It was nearly five when he left. He bought an evening paper more from habit than from any desire to read it. Suddenly he found he was tired with the staggering weariness of someone who had nothing to do but must somehow fill the hours between getting up and bedtime.

A long way back to Theresa Street on foot, too long. He hailed a taxi, sank into its seat and unfolded his paper.

From the middle of the front page the bony, almost cadaverous, face of his nephew stared back at him.

2

They set up a pillar of stone with the dead man's
titles therein engraved.

THE women were still out. Fighting the soporific heat which
had met him with a tropical blast as he entered the house,
Wexford sat down, found his new glasses, and read the
caption under the photograph. 'Detective Superintendent
Howard Fortune, Kenbourne Vale C.I.D. chief, who is in
charge of the case, arriving at Kenbourne Vale Cemetery where
the girl's body was found.'

The cameraman had caught Howard leaving his car, and it
was a full-face shot. Beneath it was another picture, macabre,
compelling the eye. Wexford, refusing to be drawn, turned his
attention to the newspaper's account of the case, its lead story.
He read it slowly.

'The body of a girl was this morning discovered in a vault
at Kenbourne Vale Cemetery, West London. It was later
identified as that of Miss Loveday Morgan, aged about 20, of
Garmisch Terrace, W.15.

'The discovery was made by Mr Edwin Tripper, of Kenbourne Lane, a cemetery attendant, when he went to give the
vault its monthly inspection. Detective Superintendent Fortune
said "This is definitely a case of foul play. I can say no more
at present."

'Mr Tripper told me, "The vault is the property of the
Monfort family who were once important people in Ken-

15

bourne. A sum of money has been set aside under a trust to keep the vault cared for but the lock on the vault door was broken many years ago.

' "This morning I went as I always do on the last Tuesday in the month to sweep out the vault and put flowers on the coffin of Mrs Viola Montfort. The door was tightly closed and jammed. I had to use tools to force it. When I got it open I went down the steps and saw the body of this girl lying between the coffins of Mrs Viola Montfort and Captain James Monfort.

' "It gave me a terrible shock. It was the last place you would expect to find a corpse".'

Wexford chuckled a little at that, but the photograph of the vault chilled him again. It was a monstrous mausoleum, erected apparently at the height of the Gothic revival. On its roof lay two vast slaughtered lions with, rampant and triumphant above them, the statue of a warrior, the whole executed in black iron. Perhaps one of the Montforts had been a big-game hunter. Beneath this set-piece, the door, worked all over with heroic frescoes, stood half open, disclosing impenetrable blackness. Ilexes, those trees beloved of cemetery architects, lowered their dusty evergreen over the vault and shrouded the warrior's head.

It was a good photograph. Both photographs were good, the one of Howard showing in his eyes that perspicacity and passionate determination every good police officer should have but which Wexford had never seen in his nephew. And never would either, he thought, laying down the paper with a sigh. He hadn't the heart to read the rest of the story. What was the betting Howard would come in for his dinner, kiss his wife, enquire what his aunt had bought and ask solicitously after his uncle's health as if nothing had happened? If anyone could ignore that evening paper, he would. It would be surreptitiously whisked away and the *status quo* would just go on and on.

But now it would be worse. Howard wouldn't really be able to pretend any longer and his continuing silence would prove what Wexford guessed already, that he thought his uncle an

16

old has-been, maybe just fit to catch a country shop-lifter or root out a band of thugs with a cock-fighting hide-out on the South Downs.

He must have fallen asleep and slept for a long time. When he awoke the paper had gone and Dora was sitting opposite him with his dinner on a tray, cold chicken, and more of those bloody biscuits and junket and two white pills.

'Where's Howard?'

'He's only just got in, darling. When he's finished his dinner he'll come in here and have his coffee with you.'

And talk about the weather?

It was, in fact, the weather on which he began.

'Most unfortunate we're having this cold spell just now, Reg.' He never called his uncle uncle and it might have caused raised eyebrows if he had, for Howard Fortune, at thirty-six, looked forty-five. People were inclined to deplore the age gap between him and his wife, not guessing it was only six years. He was exceptionally tall, extravagantly thin and his lean bony face was wrinkled, but when he smiled it became charming and almost good-looking. You could see they were uncle and nephew. The Wexford face was there, the same bone construction, though in the case of the younger man the bones were almost fleshless and in the older obscured under pouches and heavy jowls. Howard smiled now as he poured Wexford's coffee and placed it beside him.

'I see you've got *Utopia* there.'

It was not quite the remark expected of a man who has spent his day in the preliminary enquiries into murder. But Howard, in any case, didn't look the part. His silver-grey suit and lemon Beale and Inman shirt were certainly the garments he had put on that morning but they appeared as if fresh from the hands of a valet. His thin smooth fingers, handling the leather binding of More's classic, looked as if they had never handled anything harsher than old books. Having placed a cushion behind his uncle's head, he began to discourse on *Utopia*, on the 1551 Ralph Robinson translation, on More's friendship with Erasmus, occasionally pausing to insert such deferential courtesies as, 'which, of course, you already know, Reg'. He talked of other ideal societies in literature, of Andreae's *Christianopolis*, of Campanella's *City of the Sun* and of Butler's *Erewhon*. He talked pleasantly and with erudition and sometimes he broke off to allow a comment from Wexford, but Wexford said nothing.

He was boiling with anger. The man was not merely a snob, he was monstrously cruel, a sadist. To sit there lecturing like a professor on idealist philosophy when his heart must be full of its opposite, when he knew his uncle had brought in not only *Utopia* but that Dystopia on which the newspaper had enlarged. And this was the same little boy whom he, Wexford, had taught to take fingerprints!

The telephone rang and, out in the hall, Denise answered it, but Wexford could see Howard was alert for the call. He watched his nephew's face sharpen and when Denise came in to tell her husband it was for him, he saw a silent signal pass between them, a miniscule shake of the head on Howard's part indicating that the call and all it implied must be kept secret from their guest. Of course, it was one of Howard's subordinates phoning to tell him of a new development. In spite of his mortification, Wexford was hungry to know what that development could be. He listened to the murmur of Howard's voice from the hall, but he couldn't distinguish the words. It was all he could do not to open the door, and then, when Howard returned, ask him baldly. But he knew what the answer would be.

'You don't want to bother your head with all that.'

He didn't wait for Howard to come back. He took *Utopia* and made for the stairs, calling a curt good night to Denise and nodding to his nephew as he passed him. Bed was the best place for an old fogey like him. He got between the sheets and put on his glasses. Then he opened the book. His eyes felt gravelly but surely it wasn't his eye playing him a trick like that . . .? He stared and slammed the book shut.

It was in Latin.

He dreamed a lot that night. He dreamed that Howard had relented and personally driven him to Kenbourne Vale Cemetery to view with him the Montfort vault, and when he awoke it seemed impossible to him that he could go home without ever having actually seen it. The murder would, for a short space, be a topic of conversation even in Kingsmarkham. How was he going to explain to Mike that he had been excluded from all concern in it? That he had stayed with the man in charge of the case and yet learned no more than the average newspaper reader? By lying? By saying he wasn't interested? His temperament revolted from that. By telling the truth, then, that Howard had refused to confide in him.

At ten he came downstairs to the usual pantomime. Shredded wheat and orange juice and Denise waiting at the bottom of the stairs today. Otherwise it was the same as all the other mornings.

Without his having told her, Dora had discovered *Utopia* was in Latin and the two of them were already planning to get him an English translation. Denise's sister-in-law worked in a bookshop and would get him a paperback; to make assurance doubly sure, she would herself go into the library and order the Ralph Robinson.

'You needn't go to all that trouble for me,' said Wexford.

'Where are you going for your walk this morning, Uncle Reg?'

'Victoria,' he said, not adding that he was going to enquire about trains and listening in silence while they gasped about walking that distance.

Of course, he wouldn't walk. There was probably a bus. The eleven, he thought, there were always dozens of elevens except when you wanted one. Today the eleven and the twenty-two seemed to be on strike, while buses going to Kenbourne Vale charged in packs across the King's Road and up Gunter Grove.

He had a terrible urge just to see that cemetery. Howard's men would have finished with it by now, and anyone could go into cemeteries if he wanted to. Then, when he got home, he could at least describe the vault to Mike and say it was unfortunate he had to leave just at that point. Victoria station could wait. Why not phone, anyway?

The next bus said Kenbourne Lane station on its front. Wexford didn't like to ask for the cemetery in case the smiling West Indian conductor took him for another ghoulish sightseer—he was unsure of himself in London, a little of his decisive identity lost—so he said, 'All the way, please,' and settled back into his seat to pretend he was complying with that piece of hackneyed advice to tourists that the best way to see London is from the top of a bus.

Its route was up to Holland Park Avenue and then along Ladbroke Grove. Once the bus had turned into Elgin Crescent, Wexford lost his bearings. He wondered how he would know they had left North Kensington, or Notting Hill or wherever it was and entered Kenbourne Vale. The neighbourhood already fitted Crocker's description of miles of mouldering terraces, but thirty years had passed and there were tower blocks and council estates as well.

Then he saw a sign: *London Borough of Kenbourne. Copeland Hill.* All the plaques with street names on them, Copeland Terrace, Heidelberg Road, Bournemouth Grove, bore the postal direction West Fifteen.

Must be nearly there. His humiliation was giving way to excitement. The bus had lumbered round a kind of circus and entered Kenbourne Lane, a wide treeless thoroughfare, inclining upwards, a street of Asiatic food shops, squat Edwardian pubs, pawnbrokers' and small tobacconists'. He was wondering how he would find the cemetery when, as the bus came over the crown of the hill, there rose to the left of him an enormous pillared portico of yellow sandstone. Wrought-iron gates, as huge as the gates to some oriental walled city, stood open, dwarfing the workman who was touching up the black paint on their posts.

Wexford rang the bell and got off when the bus pulled in to a request stop. In this exposed place the sharp wind caught him and he turned up the collar of his coat. The heavy leaden

20

sky looked full of snow. There were no sightseers about, no police cars, and neither the workman nor some sort of attendant —Mr Tripper, perhaps?—who stood at the entrance to a lodge, said a word to him as he passed under the archway.

As soon as he was inside the cemetery, he remembered what Crocker had said about it being huge and bizarre. This was not an exaggeration, but the doctor had omitted to say that it was also, perhaps because of its size and because of staff shortages, hideously neglected. Wexford stood still and took in the sprawling wild panorama.

Immediately in front of him was one of those buildings all large cemeteries boast and whose use is in doubt. It was neither a chapel nor a crematorium, but it possibly housed offices for the staff and lavatories for the mourners. The style was that of St Peter's in Rome. Not, of course, so large, but large enough. Unluckily for the inhabitants of Kenbourne Vale, its architect had been no Bernini: the dome was too small, the pillars too thick and the whole edifice executed in the same yellow sandstone as the portico.

Of this material also were the two colonnades which branched out of the right-hand side of the St Peter's building like encircling arms and met some hundred yards distant at an arch which supported a winged victory. Between them and the outer walls, above which could be seen St Biddulph's Hospital, were deep strips of wilderness, a jungle of shrubs and trees, showing here and there protruding from the mass the weather-torn peaks of tombs.

In the space between the colonnades some attempt had been made to tidy the place. The shaggy grass was chopped off, the bushes pruned, to reveal grime-encrusted monuments, angels with swords, gun-carriages, broken columns, weeping Niobes, Egyptian obelisks and, immediately beside St Peter's, two tombs the size of small houses. Training his eyes, Wexford saw that one was that of the Princess Adelberta of Mecklenburgh-Strelitz, and the other of His Serene Highness the Grand Duke Waldemar of Retz.

The place was ridiculous, a grandiose necropolis, devour-

21

ing land which might better have served Kenbourne Vale's homeless. It was also profoundly sinister. It was awe-inspiring. Never before, not in any mortuary or house of murder, had Wexford so tellingly felt the oppressive chill of death. The winged victory held back her plunging horses against a sky that was almost black, and under the arches of the colonnades lay wells of gloom. He felt that not for anything would he have walked between those arches and the pillars which fronted them to read the bronze plaques on their damp yellow walls. Not for renewed health and youth would he have spent a night in that place.

He had mounted the steps to view the cemetery and he had viewed it. Enough was enough. Luckily, the Montfort vault must lie between the wall and the colonnade. He guessed that because only there grew the ilexes, and he was foolishly relieved to know that he would not have to explore the inner area where the most monstrous and folly-like tombs stood and where the winged victory dominated everything like some sinister fallen angel.

But as soon as he had descended the steps and taken a path which led to the right-hand side of the cemetery he found that the depths were no less unpleasant than the heights. True, the winged victory and the colonnades were made invisible by the trees, but these in themselves, crowded together, untended and almost all of evergreen varieties, held their own kind of menace. They made the path very dark. Their trunks were hidden to shoulder height by ivy and thick brambly shrubs, and among these shrubs began to appear first the outlines of gravestones and then, as the path ran parallel with the outer wall, the shapes of larger and larger tombs.

Wexford tried to chuckle at some of the pompous inscriptions but his laughter stuck in his throat. The absurd was overpowered by the sinister, by the figures in bronze and sculped stone which, made furtive and hideous by encroaching moss and decades of fallen grime, lurked among the trailing tendrils and even, as the wind rustled between leathery leaves and broken masonary, seemed to move. Overhead, he could see

22

only a narrow corridor of sky and that stormy, black and Turneresque. He walked on, looking straight ahead of him down the defile.

Just when he was beginning to feel that he had had about as much of this as flesh and blood could stand, he came upon the Montfort vault. It was the size of a small cottage and much nastier in reality than in the photograph. The cameraman had not been able to capture the mouldy smell that breathed out of the half-open door or render the peculiarly unpleasant effect of sour green moss creeping across the warrior's face and the paws of the dead lions.

Nor had the inscription appeared in the paper. It was unlike any other Wexford had seen in the cemetery, bearing no information about the dead who lay in the vault. The copper plate had turned bright green with verdigris, but the lettering, of some untarnishable metal—gold leaf?—stood out clear and stark.

'He who asks questions is a fool.
He who answers them is a greater fool.
What is truth? What man decides it shall be.
What is beauty? Beauty is in the eye of man.
What are right and wrong? Today one thing, another
    tomorrow.
Death only is real.
The last of the Montforts bids you read and pass on
Without comment.'

This epitaph—if epitaph it could be called—so interested Wexford that he took a scrap of paper and a pencil from his pocket and copied it down. Then he pushed open the door, expecting a creak, but there was no sound at all. Perhaps Mr Tripper had oiled the hinges. A creak would somehow have been reassuring. He realised suddenly that some of the awe and the disquiet he felt was due to the profound silence. Since entering the cemetery he had heard nothing but the crepitation of dead leaves beneath his feet and the rustle of the wind.

23

Inside the vault it was not quite dark. Utter darkness would have been less unpleasant. A little greyish light fell on to the flight of steps from a narrow vitrine in the rear wall. He went down the steps and found himself in a chamber about twelve feet square. The dead Montforts lay not in the coffins mentioned by Mr Tripper but in stone sarcophagi which rested on shelves. In the centre of the chamber was a marble basin absurdly like a birdbath and containing a dribble of water. He couldn't imagine what purpose it served. He approached the sarcophagi and saw that there were two rows of them with a narrow space between. It must have been there in that trough, on the damp stone floor, that Loveday Morgan's body had been found.

He shivered a little. The vault smelt of decay. Not surely of the dead Montforts, passed long ago to dust, but of rotted grave flowers and stagnant water and unventilated age. A nasty place. She had been twenty, he thought, and he hoped she had died quickly and not in here. What are right and wrong? Today one thing, another tomorrow. Death only is real.

He turned back towards the steps and, as he did so, he heard a sound above him, a footfall on the overgrown gravel path. Some attendant, no doubt. He set his foot on the bottom stair, looking up at the rectangle of dingy light between door and frame. And then, as he was about to speak and declare his presence, there appeared in the aperture, gaunt and severe, the face of his nephew.

3

*You conceive in your mind either none at all or else
a very false image and similitude of this thing.*

EVERYONE is familiar with the sensation of wanting the
earth to swallow him when he is caught in embarrassing
circumstances. And what more appropriate plot of earth than
this, thought Wexford, aghast. These acres, choked with the
dead, might surely receive one more. There was, however,
nothing for it but to mount the stairs and face the music.

Howard, peering down into semi-darkness, had not at first
recognised the intruder. When he did, when Wexford, awkwardly brushing cobwebs from his coat, emerged on to the
path, his face registered simple blank astonishment.

'Good God. Reg,' he said.

He looked his uncle up and down, then stared into the vault,
as if he thought himself the victim of some monstrous delu-
sion. Either this was not Wexford, but some Kenbournite disguised to resemble him, or else this was not Kenbourne Vale
cemetery. It took him a few moments to recover and then he
said:

'I thought you wanted a holiday from all this sort of thing.'

It was stupid to stand there like a schoolboy. In general,
embarrassment was foreign to Wexford and he brimmed over
with self-confidence. Now he told himself that he was catching
criminals when this man was chewing on a teething ring and
he said rather coldly, 'Did you? I can't imagine why.' Never

25

apologise, never explain. 'Don't let me keep you from your work. I've a bus to catch.'

Howard's eyes narrowed. 'No,' he said, 'you're not going like that.' He always spoke quietly, in measured tones. 'I won't have that. If you wanted to see the vault, why didn't you say last night? I'd have brought you with me this morning. If you wanted the inside stuff on the case, you only had to ask.'

Absurd as it was, undignified, to stand arguing in the bitter cold among toppled gravestones, Wexford couldn't leave it like that. All his resentment had boiled to the surface.

'Ask?' he shouted. 'Ask you when you've made a point of excluding me from everything to do with your work? When you and Denise have conspired to keep quiet about it like a couple of parents turning off the television in front of the child when the sexy play starts? I know when I'm not wanted. *Ask!*'

Howard's face had fallen glumly at the beginning of this speech, but now a faint smile twitched his lips. He felt in the pocket of his coat while Wexford leaned against the vault, his arms folded defiantly.

'Here, read that. It came two days before you did.' Reassured by the evidence he had produced, Howard spoke firmly now. 'Read it, Reg.'

Suspiciously Wexford took the letter. Without his glasses he could only just read it, but he could make out enough. The signature, 'Leonard Crocker', leered blackly at him. '. . . I am confident I can rely on your good sense . . . Your uncle, a close friend of mine and my patient . . . Nothing he wants more than to get completely away from everything connected with police work . . . Better not let him come into any contact with . . .'

'We thought we were acting for the best, Reg.'

'Close friend!' Wexford exploded. 'What business has he got interfering with me?' Usually litter-conscious, he forgot his principles and, screwing the letter into a ball, hurled it among the bushes and the crumbling masonry.

Howard burst out laughing. 'I spoke to my own doctor

26

about it,' he said, 'telling him what had been the matter with you and he said—you know how diplomatic they are—he said there were two opinions about it but he couldn't see that you'd come to any harm indulging—er, your usual tastes. Still, Denise insisted we abide by what your own doctor said. And we did think it was your wish.'

'I took you for a snob,' said his uncle. 'Rank and all that.'

'Did you? That never struck me.' Howard bit his lip. 'You don't know how I've longed for a real talk instead of literary chit-chat, especially now when I'm short of men and up to my eyes in it.' Frowning, still concerned, he said, 'You must be frozen. Here comes my sergeant, so we can get away from all these storeyed urns and animated busts.'

A thickset man of about forty was approaching them from the direction of St Peter's. He wore the cheerful and practical air of someone totally insensitive to atmosphere, to that of the cemetery and that which subsisted between the two other men. Howard introduced him as Sergeant Clements and presented the chief inspector without saying that Wexford was his uncle or attempting to account for his sudden and surely astonishing appearance at the scene of a crime.

In such august company the sergeant knew better than to ask questions, or perhaps he had read the Montfort injunction.

'Very pleased to meet you, sir.'

'My uncle,' said Howard, relenting a little, 'is on holiday. He comes from Sussex.'

'I daresay it's a change, sir. No green fields and cows and what-not round here.' He gave Wexford a respectful and somewhat indulgent smile before turning to the superintendent. 'I've had another talk with Tripper, sir, but I've got nothing more out of him.'

'Right. We'll go back to the car. Mr Wexford will be lunching with me, and over lunch I'm going to try to persuade him to give us the benefit of his brains.'

'We can certainly use them,' said the sergeant, and he fell back to allow the others to precede him out of the cemetery.

27

The Grand Duke was a little old pub Howard took him to on the corner of a mews in Kenbourne Lane.

'I didn't know there were places like this left in London,' Wexford said, appreciating the linenfold panelling, the settles and the old mullioned glass in the windows. It was like home, the kind of inn to be found in Pomfret or Stowerton.

'There aren't around here. Kenbourne's no Utopia. Would you believe, looking out of the window, that in an unpublished poem, Hood wrote:

' "O, to ride on the crest of a laden wain
    Between primrose banks in Kenbourne Lane"?'

'What will you eat, Reg?'

'I'm not supposed to eat anything much.'

'Surely a little cold duck and some salad? The food's very good here.'

Wexford felt almost dizzy, but he mustn't allow himself to break out entirely. It was a triumph of communication over misunderstanding that he was here with Howard at all and about to get his teeth into some real police work again without getting them into duck as well. The spread on the food counter looked mouth-wateringly enticing. He chose the least calorific, thin sliced red beef and *ratatouille froide,* and settled back with a sigh of contentment. Even the tall glass of apple juice which Howard presented to him with the assurance that it was made out of Cox's Oranges from Suffolk couldn't cloud his pleasure.

Ever since his arrival in London he had felt that partial loss of identity which is common to everybody on holiday except the most seasoned of travellers. But instead of returning to him as he grew accustomed to the city, this ego of his, this essential Wexfordness, had seemed to continue its seeping away, until at last in the cemetery he had briefly but almost entirely lost his hold on it. That had been a frightening moment. Now, however, he felt more himself than he had done for days. This was like being with Mike at the Olive and Dove where, on so many satisfactory occasions, they had thrashed

28

out some case over lunch, but now Howard was the instructor and he in Mike's role. He found he didn't mind this at all. He could even look with equanimity at Howard's lunch: a huge plateful of steak-and-kidney pudding, Jersey new potatoes and courgettes *au gratin*.

For the first five minutes they ate and drank and talked a little more about this misunderstanding of theirs, and then Howard, opening their discussion in the clearest and most direct way, pushed a snapshot across the table.

'This is the only photograph we have of her. Other may come to light, of course. It was in her handbag. Not very usual that, to carry photographs of oneself about on one. Perhaps she had some sentimental reason for it. Where and when it was taken we don't know.'

The snapshot was too pale and muzzy for reproduction in a newspaper. It showed a thin fair girl in a cotton frock and heavy unsuitable shoes. Her face was a pale blob and even her own mother, as Wexford put it to himself, wouldn't have recognised her. In the background were some dusty-looking shrubs, a section of wall with coping along the top of it and something that looked like a clothes post.

He handed it back and asked, 'Is Garmisch Terrace near here?'

'The backs of the houses overlook the cemetery but on the opposite side to where we were. It's a beastly place. Monstrous houses put up around 1870 for city merchants who couldn't run to fifteen hundred a year for a palace in Queen's Gate. They're mostly let off into rooms now, or flatlets as they're euphemistically called. She had a room. She'd lived there for about two months.'

'What did she do for a living?'

'She worked as a receptionist in a television rental place. The shop is called Sytansound and it's in Lammas Grove. That's the street which runs off to the left at Kenbourne Circus and also skirts the cemetery. Apparently she went to work by taking a short-cut through the cemetery. Why do you look like that?'

'I was thinking of passing through that place every day.'

'The local people are used to it. They don't notice it any more. You'd be surprised in the summer how many young housewives you see in there taking their babies for an afternoon's airing.'

Wexford said, 'When and how did she die?'

'Probably last Friday. I haven't had a full medical report yet, but she was strangled with her own silk scarf.'

'Last Friday and no one reported her missing?'

Howard shrugged. 'In Garmisch Terrace, Reg? Loveday Morgan wasn't living at home with her parents in some select suburb. They come and they go in Garmisch Terrace, they mind their own business, they don't ask questions. Wait till you hear Sergeant Clements on that subject.'

'How about boy friends?'

'She didn't have any, as far as we know. The body was identified by a girl called Peggy Pope who's the housekeeper at 22 Garmisch Terrace and she says Loveday had no friends. She came to Kenbourne Vale in January, but where she came from nobody seems to know. When she applied for the room she gave Mrs Pope an address in Fulham. We've checked on that. The street she named and the house she named are there all right but she never lived there. The owners of the house are a young married couple who have never let rooms. So we don't yet know where she came from and in a way we don't really know who she was.'

Having built up the suspense in a way Wexford recognised, for it was the way he had himself used on countless occasions, Howard went away to fetch cheese and biscuits. He returned with more apple juice for his uncle, who was feeling so contented that he drank it obediently.

'She lived in Garmisch Terrace by herself, very quietly,' Howard went on, 'and last Friday, February 25th, she went to work as usual, returning, as she occasionally did, during her lunchtime break. Mrs Pope supposed that she had gone back to work in the afternoon, but in fact, she didn't. She telephoned the manager of Sytansound to say she was sick and that was the last anyone heard of her.' He paused. 'She may have gone straight into the cemetery; she may not. The cemetery gates are closed each day at six, and on Fridays they were closed at that time as usual. Clements sometimes cuts through on his way home. He did that on Friday, spoke to Tripper, and Tripper closed the gates behind him at six sharp. Needless to say, Clements saw nothing out of the way. His route took him nowhere near the Montfort vault.'

Wexford recognised this short pause as the cue for him to ask an intelligent question, and he asked one. 'How did you know who she was?'

'Her handbag was beside her in the vault, brimming with information. Her address was on a bill from a dry cleaner's and this snapshot was there too. Besides that, there was a sheet of notepaper with two telephone numbers on it.'

Wexford raised an enquiring eyebrow.

'You rang those numbers, of course?'

'Of course. That was among the first things we did. One was that of an hotel in Bayswater, a perfectly respectable, rather large, hotel. They told us they had advertised in a newspaper a vacancy for a receptionist and Loveday Morgan had replied to the advertisement. By phone. She didn't sound the sort of girl they wanted—too shy and awkward, they said— and she hadn't the necessary experience for the job.

'The other number was that of a West End company called Notbourne Properties who are particularly well known in Notting Hill and Kenbourne Vale. Hence their name. They also had advertised a job, this time for a telephone girl. Loveday applied and actually got as far as an interview. That interview was at the end of the week before last, but they didn't intend to take her on. Apparently, she was badly dressed and, anyway, she wasn't familiar with the particular phone system they use.'

'She wanted to change her job? Does anyone know why?'

'More money, I imagine. We may be able to get some more information about that and her general circumstances from this Mrs Pope.'

'That's the woman who identified her? The housekeeper?'

'Yes. Shall we wait and have coffee or would you like to go straight round to Garmisch Terrace?'

'Skip the coffee,' said Wexford.

4

*A little farther beyond that all things begin by little
and little to wax pleasant; the air soft, temperate and
gentle covered with green grass.*

GARMISCH TERRACE was straight and grey and forbidding, a canyon whose sides were six-storey houses. All the houses were alike, all joined together, flat-fronted but for their protruding pillared porches, and, like the cemetery building, their proportions were somehow wrong. It had been an unhappy period for architecture, the time when they were built, a period in which those designers who had not adopted the new Gothic, were attempting to improve on the Georgian.

This would have mattered less if some effort had been made to maintain these houses, but Wexford, looking at them with a sinking heart, could not see a single freshly painted façade. Their plaster was cracked and their pillars streaked where water had run through dust. Rubbish clogged the basement areas and these were separated from the pavement by broken railings patched with wire netting. Instead of trees, parking meters stood in a grey row, an avenue of them leading up the cul-de-sac to where it ended in a red-brick church.

There were few people about, a turbaned Sikh lugging his dustbin up area steps, an old woman wheeling a pram filled apparently with jumble-sale spoils, a pregnant black girl whose kingfisher-blue raincoat provided the only colour in the street. The wind blew paper out of the Sikh's dustbin, whirling sheets of newsprint up into the grey sky. It teased at the girls woolly hair which, in a pathetic attempt to be accepted, to be in fashion, she was trying to grow long. Wexford wondered sadly about these coloured people who must have looked to a promised land and had found instead the bitter indecency of Garmisch Terrace.

'Would anyone live here from choice?' he said to Sergeant Clements, who, while Howard studied a report in the car, had attached himself to him as mentor, guide, and possibly protector.

'You may well ask, sir,' said the sergeant approvingly. His manner was not quite that of the schoolmaster addressing a promising pupil. Wexford's rank and age were recognised and respected, but he was made aware of the age-old advantage of the townsman over the greenhorn from the country. Clements' plump face, a face which seemed not to have changed much since he was a fat-cheeked, rosebud-mouthed schoolboy, wore an expression both smug and discontented. 'They like it, you see,' he explained. 'They like muck and living four to a room and chucking their gash about and prowling all night and sleeping all day.' He scowled at a young man and woman who, arm in arm, crossed the road and sat down on the pavement outside the church where they began to eat crisps out of a bag. 'They like dropping in on their friends at midnight and dossing down on the floor among the fag-ends because the last bus has gone. Ask 'em and most of 'em don't know where they live, here this week, there the next, catch as catch can and then move on. They don't live like you or me sir. They live like those little furry moles you have down in the country, always burrowing about in the dark.'

Wexford recognised in the sergeant a type of policeman which is all too common. Policemen see so much of the seamy side of life and, lacking the social worker's particular kind of training, many of them become crudely cynical instead of learning a merciful outlook. His own Mike Burden came dangerously near sometimes to being such a one, but his intelligence saved him. Wexford didn't think much of the sergeant's intelligence, although he couldn't help rather liking him.

'Poverty and misery aren't encouragements to an orderly life,' he said, smiling to take the sting out of the admonition.

Clements didn't take this as a rebuke but shook his head at so much innocence.

'I was referring to the *young*, sir, the young layabouts like that pair over there. But you'll learn. A couple of weeks in Kenbourne Vale and you'll get your eyes opened. Why, when I first came here I thought hash was mutton stew and S.T.D. a dialling system.'

Perfectly aware of the significance of these terms, Wexford said nothing, but glanced towards the car. He was beginning to feel chilly and at a nod from Howard he moved under the porch of number 22. That a lecture, contrasting the manners of modern youth with the zeal, ambition and impeccable morality of Clements' contemporaries in his own young days, was imminent he felt sure, and he hoped to avoid. But the sergeant followed him, stamping his feet on the dirty step, and launched into the very diatribe Wexford most feared. For a couple of minutes he let him have his head and then he interrupted.

'About Loveday Morgan . . .'

'So-called,' said Clements darkly. 'That wasn't her real name. Now, I ask you, is it likely to be? We checked her at Somerset House. Plenty of Morgan girls but no Loveday Morgan. She just called herself that. Why? You may well ask. Girls call themselves all sorts of things these days. Now, let me give you an illustration of what I mean . . .'

But before he could, Howard had joined them and silenced him with an unusually cold look. There was a row of bells beside the front door with numbers instead of nameplates.

'The housekeeper lives in the basement,' said Howard, 'so we may as well try Flat One.' He rang the bell and a voice snapped what sounded like 'Teal' out of the entry phone.

35

'I beg your pardon?'

'This is Ivan Teal. Flat One. Who are you?'

'Detective Superintendent Fortune. I want Mrs Pope.'

'Ah,' said the voice. 'You want Flat Fifteen. The thing that works the door is broken. I'll come down.'

'Flats!' said the sergeant while they waited. 'That's a laugh. They aren't any of 'em flats. They're rooms with a tap and a gas meter, but our girl was paying seven quid a week for hers and there are only two loos in the whole dump. What a world!' He patted Wexford's shoulder. 'Brace yourself for what's coming now, sir. Whoever this Teal is he won't look human.'

But he did. The only shock Wexford felt was in confronting a man nearly as old as himself, a shortish, well-muscled man with thick grey hair worn rather long.

'Sorry to keep you waiting,' he said. 'It's a long way down.' He stared at the three men, unsmiling, insolent in a calculating way. It was a look Wexford had often seen on faces before, but they had almost always been young faces. Teal had, moreover, a smooth upper-class accent. He wore a spotlessly clean white sweater and smelt of Faberge's Aphrodisia. 'I suppose we're all going to be persecuted now.'

'We don't persecute people, Mr Teal.'

'No? You've changed then. You used to persecute me.'

Assuming that Howard had given him *carte blanche* to question possible witnesses if he chose, Wexford said, 'Did you know Loveday Morgan?'

'I know everybody here,' Teal said, 'the oldest inhabitants and the ships that pass in the night. I who have sat by Thebes below the wall . . .' He grinned suddenly. 'Flat One if you want me.'

He led them to the basement stairs and went off without saying any more.

'A curious old queen,' said Howard. 'Fifteen years in this hole . . . God! Come on, it's down here.'

The stairs were narrow and carpeted in a thin much-worn haircord. They led down to a largish lofty hall, long ago painted dark crimson, but this paint was peeling away, leaving white islands shaped like fantastic continents, so that the walls might have been maps of some other unknown world, a charted Utopia. Furniture, that looked too big to go up those stairs although it must have come down them, a sideboard, a huge bookcase crammed with dusty volumes, filled most of the floor space. There were three closed doors, each with an overflowing dustbin on its threshold, and the place smelt of decaying rubbish.

Wexford had never seen anything like this before, but the interior of Flat Fifteen was less unfamiliar. It reminded him of certain Kingsmarkham cottages he had been in. Here was the same squalor that is always present when edibles and washables are thrown into juxtaposition, opened cans among dirty socks, and here in one of those battered prams was a baby with a food-stained face such as town and country alike produce. It was deplorable, of course, that this young girl and her child should have to live in a subterranean cavern, perpetually in artificial light; on the other hand, daylight would have revealed even more awfully the broken armchairs and the appalling carpet. In a way, this was a work of art, so carefully had some female relative of the landlord's repaired it. Wexford couldn't tell whether it was a blue carpet mended with crimson or a piece of red weaving incorporating patches of blue Axminster. The whole of it was coated with stains, ground-in food and the housekeeper's hair combings.

She alone of the room's contents could have stood up to the searching light of day. Her clothes were awful, as dirty and dilapidated as the chair coverings, and dust clung to her greasy black hair, but she was beautiful. She was easily the most beautiful woman he had seen since he came to London. Hers was the loveliness of those film stars he remembered from his youth in the days before actresses looked like ordinary women. In her exquisite face he saw something of a Carole Lombard, something of a Loretta Young. Sullen and dirty though she was, he could not take his eyes off her.

Howard and Clements seemed totally unaffected. No doubt

37

they were too young to have his memories. Perhaps they were too efficient to be swayed by beauty. And the girl's manner didn't match her looks. She sat on the arm of a chair, biting her nails and staring at them with a sulky frown.

'Just a few questions, please, Mrs Pope,' said Howard.

'Miss Pope. I'm not married.' Her voice was rough and low. 'What d'you want to know? I can't spare very long. I've got the bins to take up if Johnny doesn't come back.'

'Johnny?'

'My friend that I live with.' She cocked a thumb in the direction of the baby and said, 'Her father. He said he'd come back and help me when he'd got his Social Security, but he always makes himself bloody scarce on bin day. God, I don't know why I don't meet up with any ordinary people, nothing but layabouts.'

'Loveday Morgan wasn't a layabout.'

'She had a job, if that's what you mean.' The baby had begun to grizzle. Peggy Pope picked up a dummy from the floor, wiped it on her cardigan and thrust it into the child's mouth. 'God knows how she kept it, she was so *thick*. She couldn't make her meter work and had to come to me to know where to buy a light bulb. When she first came here I even had to show her how to make a phone call. Oh, they all impose on me, but never the way she did. And then she had the nerve to try and get Johnny away from me.'

'Really?' said Howard encouragingly. 'I think you should tell us that, Mrs Pope.'

'*Miss* Pope. Look, I've got to get the bins up. Anyway, there wasn't anything in it, not on Johnny's side. Loveday was so bloody obvious about it, always coming down here to chat him up when I was out, and it got worse the last couple of weeks. I'd come back and find her sitting here, staring at Johnny, or making out she was fond of the baby. I asked him what she was up to. What d'you talk about, for God's sake? I said. Nothing, he said. She'd hardly opened her mouth. She was such a bloody miserable sort of girl.' Peggy Pope sighed as

38

if she, the soul of wit and gaiety, had a right to similarly exuberant companions.

'Do you know why she was miserable?'

'It's money with most of them. That's all they talk about, as though I was rolling in it. She asked me if I could find her a cheaper room, but I said, No, I couldn't. We don't have any flats less than seven a week. I thought she was going to cry. Christ, I thought, why don't you grow up?'

Howard said, 'May we come to last Friday, Mrs Pope?'

'*Miss* Pope. When I want to be *Mrs* I'll find a man who's got a job and can get me something better than a hole in the ground to live in, I can tell you. I don't know anything about last Friday. I saw her come in about ten past one and go off again about ten to two. Oh, and she made a phone call. I don't know any more about it.'

Wexford caught Howard's eye and leant forward. 'Miss Pope,' he said, 'we want you to tell us about that in much greater detail. Tell us exactly what you were doing, where you saw her, what she said, everything.'

'O.K., I'll try.' Peggy Pope pulled her thumbnail out of her mouth and looked at it with distaste. 'But when I've done you'll have to let me get shifting those bins.'

The room was rather cold. She kicked down the upper switch on an electric fire and a second bar began to heat. It was evidently seldom used, for as it glowed red a smell of burning dust came from it.

'It was just after one, maybe ten past,' she began. 'Johnny was out somewhere as usual, looking for work, he said, but I reckon he was in the Grand Duke. I was in the hall giving it a bit of a sweep up and Loveday came in. She said hallo or something, and I said hallo, and she went straight upstairs. I was getting out the vacuum when she came down again and said had I got change for ten pence because she wanted two pence to make a phone call. She must have known I don't carry money about when I'm cleaning the place, but, anyway, I said I'd see and I came down here and got my bag. I hadn't got change, but I'd got one two-pence piece so I gave her that and she went into the phone box.'

'Where's that?'

'Under the stairs. You passed it when you came down.'

'Do you know whom she was phoning?'

She warmed her bitten fingers at the fire and creased her beautiful face into a ferocious scowl. 'How would I? There's a door on the box. She didn't say I'm going to give my mother a tinkle or ring my boy friend, if that's what you mean. Loveday never said much. I'll give her that, she wasn't talkative. Well, she came out and went upstairs again and then I went down to see if the baby was O.K., and when I came up with the pram to take the washing to the launderette she was just going out through the front door, all got up in a green trouser suit. I noticed because it was the only decent thing she had. She didn't say anything. And now can I get on with my work?'

Howard nodded, and he and Clements, thanking her briefly, made for the stairs. Wexford lingered. He watched the girl—she was round-shouldered and rather thin—lift one of the smelly bins and then he said, 'I'll give you a hand.'

She seemed astonished. The world she lived in had unfitted her for accepting help graciously, and she shrugged, making her mouth into an ugly shape.

'They should employ a man to do this.'

'Maybe, but they don't. What man would practically run this dump and do all the dirty work for eight quid a week and that room? Would *you*?'

'Not if I could help it. Can't you get a better job?'

'Look, chum, there's the kid. I've got to have a job where I can look after her. Don't you worry yourself about me. Some day my prince will come and then I'll be off out of here, leaving the bins to Johnny.' She smiled for the first time, a transcending, glorious smile, evoking for him old dark cinemas and shining screens. 'Thanks very much. That's the lot.'

'You're welcome,' said Wexford.

The unaccustomed effort had brought the blood beating to his

40

head. It had been a silly thing to do and the pounding inside his temples unnerved him. Howard and the sergeant were nowhere to be seen, so, to clear his head while he waited for them, he walked down to the open end of Garmisch Terrace. A thin drizzle had begun to fall. He found himself in something which at home would have passed for a high street. It was a shabby shopping centre with, sandwiched between a pub and a hairdresser's, a little cheap boutique called *Loveday*. So that was where she had found the name. She had possessed some other, duller perhaps but identifying, distressing even, which she had wished to conceal. . . .

'Been having a breath of fresh air, sir?' said the sergeant when he rejoined them. 'Or what passes for it round here. By gum, but those bins stank to high heaven!'

Howard grinned. 'We'll take the sergeant back to the station and then I want to show you something different. You mustn't run away with the idea that the whole of Kenbourne is like these rat holes.'

They dropped Clements at the police station, a blackened pile in Kenbourne Vale High Street whose blue lamp swung from the centre of an arch above an imposing flight of steps. Then Howard, driving the car himself, swung into a hinterland of slums, winding streets with corner shops and pubs and patches of waste ground, once green centres of garden squares, but now wired-in like hard tennis courts and littered with broken bicycles and oil-drums.

'Clements lives up there.' Howard pointed upwards, apparently through the roof of the car, and, twisting round to peer out of the window, Wexford saw a tower block of flats, a dizzy thirty storeys. 'Quite a view, I believe. He can see the river and a good deal of the Thames Estuary on a clear day.'

Now the towers grew thickly around them, a copse of monoliths sprouting out of a shabby and battered jungle. Wexford was wondering if this was the contrast he had expected to admire when a bend in the road brought them suddenly to a clear open space. The change was almost shocking. A second before

41

he had been in one of the drabbest regions he had ever set eyes on, and now, as if a scene had been rapidly shifted on a stage, he saw a green triangle, plane trees, a scattering of Georgian houses. Such, he supposed, was London, ever variable, constantly surprising.

Howard pulled up in front of the largest of these houses, cream-painted, with long gleaming windows and fluted columns supporting the porch canopy. There were flower-beds and on each side of the house carefully planned layouts of cypresses and pruned kanzans. A notice fixed to the wall read: *Vale Park. Strictly Private. Parking for Residents only. By order of Notbourne Properties Ltd.*

'The old Montfort house,' said Howard, 'owned by the company to whom Loveday applied for a job.'

'The paths of glory,' said his uncle, 'lead but to the grave. What became of the Montforts, apart from the grave?'

'I don't know. The man to tell you would be Stephen Dearborn, the chairman of Notbourne Properties. He's supposed to be a great authority on Kenbourne Vale and its history. The company have bought up a lot of places in Kenbourne and they've done a good job smartening them up.'

It was unfortunate, Wexford thought, that they hadn't operated on Kenbourne Vale police station. It was in acute need of renovation, of pale paint to modify the gloom of bottle-green walls, mahogany woodwork and dark passages. One of these vaulted corridors led to Howard's own office, a vast chamber with a plum-red carpet, metal filing cabinets and a view of a brewery. The single bright feature of the room was human and female, a girl with a copper beech hair and surely the longest legs in London.

She looked up from the file she was studying as they entered and said, 'Mrs Fortune's been on the phone for you, sir. She said please would you call her back as it's very urgent.'

'Urgent, Pamela? What's wrong?' Howard moved to the phone.

'Apparently your . . .' The girl hesitated. 'Your uncle that's

42

staying with you is missing. He went out five hours ago and he hasn't come back. Mrs Fortune sounded very worried.'

'My God,' said Wexford. 'I was going to Victoria station. I shall be in terribly deep water.'

'You and me both,' said Howard, and then they began to laugh.

5

*They gladly hear also the young men, yea, ana pur-
posely provoke them to talk . . .*

'Aunt Dora,' said Denise icily, 'is lying down. When
her headache is better we're going over to my brother's
to play bridge.'

Wexford made a further attempt to placate her. 'I'm very
sorry about all this, my dear. I didn't mean to upset you, but
it went right out of my head.'

'Please don't worry about me. It's Aunt Dora who's upset.'

'Men must work and women must weep,' said Howard
rather unkindly. 'Now, where's my dinner and his snack?'

'I'm afraid I didn't prepare anything special for Uncle Reg.
You see, we thought that since he seems to be disregarding all
his doctor's warnings . . .'

'You'd punish him by giving him a proper meal? Poor old
Reg. It looks as if we shall have to deal with you as More
dealt with the children in Utopia, by letting them stand and
be fed from the master's plate.'

Dora's manner, when she came down, was injured and
distrait, but the chief inspector had been married for thirty
years and had seldom permitted petticoat government.

Observing the determined gleam in his eye, she contented
herself with a piteous, 'Oh, darling, how *could* you?' before
sallying forth to her bridge game.

'Let's go into my study,' Howard said when they had finished their pilaf. 'I want to talk to you about that phone call.'

The study was a lot pleasanter than Howard's office in Kenbourne Vale and its appointments less vulnerable than those in the feminine-dominated part of the house. Wexford took his seat by a window through which could be seen, by way of a narrow opening between house backs, the flash of lights passing eternally down the King's Road. He was not yet used to living in a place where it never grew dark and where all night the sky held a plum-red glow.

'You look much better, Reg,' Howard said, smiling. 'May I say that ten years have fallen away from you in the space of one afternoon?'

'I daresay. One doesn't like to take a back seat, to live vicariously.' Wexford sighed. 'The tragedy of growing old is not that one is old but that one is young.'

'I've always thought *Dorian Gray* a very silly book and that epigram one of its few redeeming features. *And* it comes nearly on the last page.'

'Literary chit-chat, Howard?'

His nephew laughed. 'Not another word,' he said. 'Now that phone call Loveday made from Garmisch Terrace . . .'

'It was to Sytansound, wasn't it? You said she phoned Sytansound to say she was sick.'

'So she did, but that call was made at two o'clock and the one from Garmisch Terrace at one-fifteen. Whom did she phone?'

'Her mother? An old aunt? A girl friend? Perhaps she was replying to one of those advertisements.' When Howard shook his head at that, Wexford said, 'You're sure the call to Sytansound wasn't made earlier?'

'The manager took it, a man called Gold, and he's positive Loveday didn't phone before two. She was due back at two and he was beginning to wonder where she was when the phone rang.'

'She made one call from home but the other from a call box outside? Why?'

'Oh, surely because she had no more change. Don't you remember the Pope woman said Loveday asked her for change but all she had was one two-pence piece? Loveday must have got change outside, bought some cigarettes or a bar of chocolate and then gone into a phone box.'

'Yes, the first call was the decisive one, the important one On the outcome of that depended whether she returned to work or not. It was made to her killer.' Wexford rubbed his eye, caught himself doing it and relaxed. It was easy to relax now that he was being admitted to the secret sanctum of Howard's house and, better than that, the sanctum of his thoughts. 'Tell me about the Sytansound people,' he said.

Believing that the passing lights troubled his uncle, Howard drew the curtains and began. 'Gold is a man of sixty,' he said. 'He has a flat over the shop and he was in the shop all Friday afternoon. At five-thirty he switched the phone over to the answering service and went upstairs where he remained all the evening. That's well corroborated. Also at Sytansound are two reps and two engineers. The two reps and one of the engineers are married and live out of Kenbourne. The other is a boy of twenty-one. Their movements are being checked, but, if we're assuming that whoever received that phone call is Loveday's killer, it wasn't any of the older ones. They were all in the Lammas Arms from one till ten to two and none left the table to take a phone call. The twenty-one-year-old was putting a new valve in a television set at a house in Copeland Road. It may be worth checking as to whether anyone phoned that house while he was there, although it seems unlikely. As far as we know, Loveday had hardly ever spoken to the reps and the engineers. Listen, this is from Gold's statement.'

Howard had brought his briefcase into the study with him. He opened it and sorted out one sheet of paper from a small stack. ' "She was very quiet and polite. She was popular with the customers because she was always polite and patient. You would not call her the kind of girl who would ever stick up for herself. She was old-fashioned. When she first came she wore no make-up and I had to ask her to." Apparently, he also asked her to turn her skirts up a bit and not to wear the same clothes every day.'

'What wages did he pay her?'

'Twelve pounds a week. Not much, was it, when you remember she was paying seven for her room? But the job was quite unskilled. All she had to do was show people two or three types of television set and ask for their names and addresses. The reps deal with the rental forms and take the money.'

Wexford bit his lip. It troubled him to think of this quiet polite girl, a child to him, living among the Peggy Popes of this world and paying more than half her wages for a room in Garmisch Terrace. He wondered how she had filled her evenings when, after walking from work through the gloomy defiles of the cemetery, she let herself into a cell perhaps twelve feet by twelve, a private vault for the living. No friends, no money to spend, no kind lover, no nice clothes . . .

'What was in her room?' he asked.

'Very little. A couple of sweaters, a pair of jeans, one dress, a topcoat. I don't think I've ever been in a room occupied by a girl and found so little evidence that a girl had ever occupied it. What little sticks of make-up she had were in her handbag. There was a cake of soap in the room, a bottle of shampoo, two or three women's magazines and a Bible.'

'A *Bible*?'

Howard shrugged. 'It may not have been hers, Reg. There was no name in it and the room was furnished—so-called, as Clements would say. It's possible the Bible was left behind by a previous tenant or that it just drifted there from some hoard of old books. There was a bookcase in the basement, if you noticed. Peggy Pope didn't know if it was hers or whose it was.'

'Will you try to find her parents?'

'We *are* trying. Of course, we haven't a proper photograph but all the newspapers have carried detailed descriptions. They must show themselves in the next couple of days if they're still alive, and why shouldn't they be? They wouldn't have to be more than in their forties.'

Wexford said carefully, 'Would you mind if tomorrow I sort of poke about a bit at Garmisch Terrace, talk to people and so on?'

'Poke about all you like,' Howard said affectionately. 'I need your help, Reg.'

Wexford was up by seven-thirty, bent on leaving by car with Howard, and this defiance sent both women into a flurry. Dora had only just come downstairs and there had been no time to prepare a special breakfast for him.

'Just boil me an egg, my dear,' he said airily to Denise, 'and I'll have a cup of coffee.'

'If you hadn't worried us nearly to death yesterday, we'd have gone out and bought you some of that Austrian cereal with the dried fruit and the extra vitimins.'

Wexford shuddered and helped himself surreptitiously to a slice of white bread.

'Your pills,' said his wife, trying to sound cold. 'Oh, Reg,' she wailed suddenly, 'carry them with you and please, please, don't forget to take them!'

'I won't,' said Wexford, pocketing the bottle.

The rush-hour traffic was heavy and nearly forty minutes elapsed before Howard dropped him outside 22 Garmisch Terrace. The pavements were wet and darkly glittering. As he slammed the car door, he saw a black-caped figure come out of the church and scurry off towards the shops.

The only living creature visible, apart from a cat peering through a grating into sewer depths, was a young man who sat on the top step of number 22, reading a copy of *The Stage*.

'The entry phone doesn't work,' he said as Wexford approached.

'I know.'

'I'll let you in if you like,' said the young man with the lazy indifference of the Frog Footman. He looked, if no means

48

of entering had been available, capable of sitting there until tomorrow. But he had a key, or said he had, and he proceeded to search for it through the pockets of a smelly Afghan jacket. In fashionable usage, Wexford decided, he would be termed one of the Beautiful People, and if like went to like, this must be Johnny.

'I believe you were friendly with the dead girl,' he said.

'Don't know about friendly. I sort of knew her. You the police?'

Wexford nodded. 'You're called Johnny. What's your other name?'

'Lamont.' Johnny wasn't disposed to be talkative. He found his key and let them into the hall where he stood gazing rather moodily at the chief inspector, a lock of dark chestnut hair falling over his brow. He was certainly very handsome with the look of an unkempt and undernourished Byron.

'Who was she friendly with in this house?'

'Don't know,' said Johnny. 'She said she hadn't any friends.' He seemed even more gloomy and indifferent than Peggy Pope and a good deal less communicative. 'She never spoke to anyone here but Peggy and me.' With a kind of lugubrious satisfaction he added: 'No one here can tell you anything. Besides, they'll all be at work by now.' He shrugged heavily, stuffed his magazine into his pocket and shambled off towards the basement stairs.

Wexford took the upward flight. Johnny had been correct in his assumption that most of the tenants would be out at work. He had expected the door of Loveday's room to be sealed up, but it stood ajar. Two plain-clothes men and one in uniform stood by the small sash window talking in low voices. Wexford paused and looked curiously into the room. It was very small and very bare, containing only a narrow bed, a chest of drawers and a bentwood chair. One corner, curtained off with a strip of thin yellow cretonne, provided storage space for clothes. The view from the window was of a plain and uncompromising brick wall, the side evidently of a deep well between this house and the one next door. The well acted

as a sounding box, and the cooing of a pigeon perched somewhere higher up came to Wexford's ears as a raucous and
hollow bray.

One of the men, seeing him and taking him for a sightseer,
stepped briskly over and slammed the door. He went on up.
On the third floor he found two tenants at home, an Indian
whose room smelt of curry and joss-sticks and a girl who said
she worked in a nightclub. Neither had ever spoken to Loveday Morgan but they remembered her as self-effacing, quiet and
sad. Somewhat breathless by now, he reached the top of the
fourth flight, where he encountered Peggy Pope, a pile of bed-
linen in her arms, talking to a girl with a plain but vivacious
face.

'Oh, it's you,' said Peggy. 'Who let you in?'

'Your friend Johnny.'

'Oh God, he's supposed to be down the Labour. He'll just
lie about in bed now till the pubs open. I don't know what's
got into him lately, he's going to pieces.'

The other girl giggled.

'Did you know Loveday Morgan?' Wexford asked her
sharply.

'I said hallo to her once or twice. She wasn't my sort. The
only time I really talked to her was to ask her to a party
I was giving. That's right, isn't it, Peggy?'

'I reckon.' Peggy turned dourly to Wexford. 'She has a
party every Saturday night and a bloody awful row they make.
Sets my kid off screaming half the night.'

'Come off it, Peggy. You know you and Johnny have a
great time at my parties.'

'Did Loveday accept your invitation?' Wexford asked.

'Of course not. She looked quite shocked like as if I'd asked
her to an orgy. Mind you, she was very nice about it. She
said not to worry about the noise. She liked to hear people
enjoying themselves, but I thought, well, you're more like an
old aunt than a kid of twenty.'

'She'd got no life in her at all,' said Peggy with a heavy
sigh.

At the top of the last flight Wexford had much the same sensation as he had received when coming from the dingy wastes of Kenbourne into the light and space which surrounded the Montfort house. The arch at the head of the stairs had been filled in with a glass door set in a frame of polished wood and from this frame, hooked to white trellis, hung a display of house plants. These were so well arranged and well tended as to have satisfied even Denise.

The air smelt cleaner, fresher. Wexford stood still for a moment, getting his breath back, and then he put his finger to the bell above a small plaque which read: *'Chez* Teal.'

6

There be divers kinds of religion not only in sundry parts of the island, but also in divers places of every city

'I THOUGHT you'd turn up sooner or later,' said Ivan Teal. The look he gave Wexford was not the insolent stare of the previous day, but slightly mocking, containing a kind of intense inner amusement. 'Come in. You seem rather out of breath. Perhaps you've been afraid to breathe in case you might inhale something nasty? The stairs do smell, don't they? There must be some very unusual germs lurking in those cracks. I'm sure they'd be a source of fascination to a bacteriologist.' He closed the door and continued to talk in the same light indulgent tone. 'You may wonder why I live here. In point of fact, it has its advantages. The view, for instance, and I have plenty of space for a low rent. Besides, I'm sure you'll agree I've made the flat rather nice.'

It would have seemed nice in any surroundings. Here it was like a jewel in a pigsty. Apart from being spotlessly clean, the flat was decorated with an artist's taste in intense clear colours, the carpets deep, the walls hung here and there with abstract paintings. Wexford walked ahead of Teal into a long lounge running the length of the back of the house. The small sash windows had been removed and replaced by a fifteen-foot-long sheet of plate glass through which could be seen, starkly and almost indecently, the full windswept panorama of Kenbourne Cemetery. He stepped back, disconcerted, and saw

Teal's lips twitch.

'Our guest thinks we have an unhealthy taste for the macabre,' he said. 'Perhaps, child, we should get some pretty little lace curtains.'

Wexford had been so drawn to the window that he had not noticed the boy who knelt on the floor beside a wall-length well-stocked bookcase. As Teal addressed him, he got up and stood awkwardly, fidgeting with the girdle of his towelling dressing gown. He was perhaps twenty-two, slim, fair, with huge rather dull eyes.

'Let me introduce Philip Chell, the other consenting adult in this establishment.' Teal's twitching mouth broke into a grin. 'You've no idea what a pleasure it is to say that openly to a policeman.'

'Oh, Ivan!' said the boy.

'Oh, *Ivan*!' Teal mocked. 'There's nothing to be afraid of. We're doing nothing wrong. At your age you can surely hardly remember when it *was* wrong.' Still smiling, but rather less pleasantly, he said to Wexford, 'Unlike me who have suffered much from policemen.' He shrugged in the boy's direction. 'We must let bygones be bygones and give him some coffee. Go and get it, child.'

Philip Chell went with a sulky flounce.

Teal stared out at the cemetery, his head slightly on one side. 'I'm badly hung-up about it, aren't I? Shall I tell you a joke? It's quite proper, though you might not think so from the way it starts.' He turned his pale grey insolent eyes full on Wexford's face. 'Three men, an Englishman, a Frenchman and a Russian. Each tells the others what gives him the greatest pleasure. The Englishman says cricket on the village green on a fine Saturday afternoon in June. A bowl of bouillabaisse made by *une vraie Marseillaise,* says the Frenchman. It is night, says the Russian, I am in my flat. There comes a knock at my door the secret police are outside, soft hats, raincoats concealing guns. And my greatest pleasure comes when they ask for Ivan Ivanovitch and I can tell them that Ivan Ivanovitch lives next door.'

53

Wexford laughed.

'But you see, my friend, I wasn't able to say that, for Ivan lived here. And on two occasions I had to go with them.' His voice changed and he said lightly. 'Now my pleasure is to have policemen in for coffee. You know, one advantage the straight has over the gay is that he has a woman in the house and women are better at chores. That boy's hopeless. Make yourself at home while I go and rescue him.'

The bookshelves contained Proust, Gide and Wilde, as he might have expected, and a lot more he didn't expect. If Teal had read all these books Teal was well read. He reached for a calf-bound volume and, as he did so, its owner's voice said at his elbow:

'John Addington Symonds? Isn't he rather old-hat? Poor fellow. Swinburne called him Mr Soddington Symonds, you know.'

'I didn't know,' said Wexford, laughing, 'and I don't want Symonds. I see you've Robinson's translation of *Utopia*.'

'Borrow it.' Teal took the book down and handed it to Wexford. 'Do you take cream with your coffee? No? My friend has retired to the bedroom. I think he's afraid I'm going to make all sorts of revelations to you.'

'I hope you are, Mr Teal, though not of a kind that would embarrass Mr Chell. I want you to talk to me about Loveday Morgan.'

Teal placed himself on the window-seat, resting one arm along the sill. Sitting down, Wexford couldn't see the cemetery. Teal's face, one of those polished brown faces, both youthless and ageless, was framed against the milky sky. 'I knew her only very slightly,' he said. 'She was a strange repressed child. She had that look about her of a person who had been brought up by strict old-fashioned parents. Once or twice on Sunday mornings I saw her go off to church, go creeping off as if she were doing something both wrong and irresistible.'

'To *church*?' Suddenly he remembered the Bible. It had been hers then, after all.

'Why not?' exclaimed Teal, his voice loud and impatient.

'Some people still go to church even in these enlightened times.'

'Which church?'

'That one up at the end of the street, of course. I wouldn't have known she was going to church if she'd been trotting off to St Paul's, would I?'

'You needn't get so heated,' Wexford said mildly. 'Is that place C. of E.? No, I shouldn't think so.'

'They call themselves the Children of the Revelation. They're rather like Exclusives or Plymouth Bretheren. There's this chapel—temple, they call it—and another one up north somewhere and one in South London. Surely you as a policeman remember the fuss a year or two back when one of their ministers was up in court for some sort of indecency. Poor sod. It was in all the papers.' He added reflectively, 'It always is.'

'Was Loveday a—er, Child of the Revelation?'

'Hardly. She worked in a television shop, and to them television, newspapers and films are synonymous with sin. She probably went there because it was the nearest church and she wanted some comfort. I never discussed it with her.'

'What did you discuss with her, Mr Teal?'

'I'm coming to that. More coffee?' He refilled Wexford's cup and stretched out his legs, yawning. 'She was a quiet, sad sort of a girl as I daresay you've gathered. I don't think I'd ever seen her smile or look cheerful until one day about a fortnight ago. It was February the 14th, if that's any help to you. I remember'—he smiled sourly—'because that idiot child Philip had seen fit to send me a Valentine and we had a row about it. Sentimental nonsense! Well, instead of going out with him as we'd arranged, I was going for a quiet drink on my own to the Queen's Arms when I met Loveday coming along Queen's Lane—that's the street at the bottom here, in case you didn't know—looking as if she'd come into a fortune. It was just before six and she was on her way home from work. I'd never seen her looking the way she looked that evening. She was almost laughing, like a child laughs, you know, from joy.'

55

Wexford nodded. 'Go on.'

'She almost bumped into me. She didn't know where she was going. I asked her if she was all right and she stopped smiling and gave me a rather a stunned look. For a moment I thought she was going to faint. "Are you all right?" I said again. "I don't know," she said. "I feel funny. I don't know what I feel, Mr Teal. I'd like to sit down." Anyway, the upshot of it was I took her into the Queen's Arms and bought her a brandy. She was rather reluctant about that, but she didn't seem to have much resistance left. I don't think she'd ever had brandy before. The colour came back into her face, what colour she ever had, and I thought she'd open her heart to me.'

'But she didn't?'

'No. She looked as if she wanted to. She couldn't. Years of repression had made it impossible for her to confide in anyone. Instead she began asking me about Johnny and Peggy Pope. Were they trustworthy? Did I think Johnny would stay with Peggy? I couldn't tell her. They've only been here four months, not much longer than Loveday herself. I asked her in what way trustworthy, but she only said, "I don't know." Then I brought her back here and the only other time I ever spoke to her was last week when she asked me about Johnny and Peggy again. She wanted to know if they were very poor.'

'Strange question. She couldn't have helped them financially.'

'Certainly not. She hadn't any money.'

'What does Lamont do for a living?'

'Peggy told me he's a bricklayer by trade but that kind of work spoils the hands, if you please, and our Johnny has ambitions to act. He did a bit of modelling once and since then he's had some very grandiose ideas about his future. He's scared Peggy'll leave him and take the baby, but not scared enough apparently to settle down to a job of work. I imagine Loveday was a bit in love with him but he wouldn't have looked at her. Peggy's quite dazzlingly beautiful, don't you think, in spite of the dirt?'

Wexford agreed, thanking Teal for the coffee and the information, although it had let in little daylight.

The bedroom door moved slightly as they came out into the hall.

'She had no friends, no callers?' Wexford asked.

'I wouldn't know.' Teal eyed the door narrowly, then flung it open. 'Come out of there, child! There's no need to eavesdrop.'

'I wasn't eavesdropping, Ivan.' In the interim the boy had dressed himself in a scarlet sweater and velvet trousers. He looked pretty and he smelt of toilet water. 'I *do* live here,' he said sulkily. 'You shouldn't shut me up.'

'Perhaps Mr Chell can help us.' Wexford did his best not to laugh.

'As a matter of fact, maybe I can.' Chell turned a coquettish shoulder in Teal's direction and gave the chief inspector a winning smile. 'I saw a girl looking for Loveday.'

'When was that, Mr Chell?'

'Oh, I don't know. Not very long ago. She was young. She came in a car, a red Mini. I was going out and this girl was standing on the step, looking at the bells. She said she'd rung at Flat Eight but the young lady seemed to be out. Funny thing for one girl to say about another, wasn't it? The young lady? Then Loveday came along the street and said hallo to her and took her upstairs with her.'

Teal looked piqued. He seemed put out because Chell had told Wexford so much and he had told him so little. 'Well, describe this girl, child,' he said pettishly. 'Describe her. You see, Mr Wexford, that here we have a close observer who looks quite through the deeds of men.'

Wexford ignored him. 'What was she like?'

'Not exactly "with it", if you know what I mean.' The boy giggled. 'She'd got short hair and she was wearing a sort of dark blue coat Oh, and *gloves*,' he added as if these last were part of some almost unheard-of tribal paraphernalia.

'A full and detailed portrait,' sneered Teal. 'Never mind what colour her eyes were or if she were five feet or six feet tall. She wore *gloves*. Now all you have to do is find a conventional young lady who wears gloves and there's your murderer. Hey presto! Run along, now, back to your mirror. Be good, sweet child, and let who will be clever!'

It wasn't until Wexford was out in the street that he realised he had left *Utopia* lying on Teal's table. Let it stay there. He didn't relish the thought of climbing all those stairs again to fetch it and perhaps intruding into the monumental row he guessed had broken out between the two men. Instead, he walked to the limit of the cul-de-sac where two stumpy stone posts sprouted out of the pavement and eyed the strange ugly church.

Like Peggy Pope's clothes, every item which went to make up this unprepossessing whole seemed chosen with a deliberate eye to the hideous. What manner of man, or group of men, he asked himself, had designed this building and seen it as fit for the worship of their God? It was hard to say when it had been built. There was no trace of the Classical or the Gothic in its architecture, no analogy with any familiar style of construction. It was squat, shabby and mean. Perhaps in some seamy depths at its rear there were windows, but here at the front there was only a single circle of red glass not much bigger than a bicycle wheel, set under a rounded gable of port-coloured brick. Scattered over the whole façade was a noughts and crosses pattern of black and ochre bricks among the red.

The door was small and such as might have been attached to a garden shed. Wexford tried it but it was locked. He stooped down to read the granite tablet by this door: *Temple of the Revelation. The Elect shall be Saved.*

The hand which descended with a sharp blow on his shoulder made him wheel round.

'Go away,' said the bearded man in black. 'No trespassers here.'

'Kindly take your hand off my coat,' Wexford snapped.

Perhaps unused to any kind of challenge, the man did as he was told. He glared at Wexford, his eyes pale and fanatical. 'I don't know you.'

'That doesn't give you the right to assault me. I know you. You're the minister of this lot.'

'The Shepherd. What do you want?'

'I'm a police officer investigating the murder of Miss Loveday Morgan.'

The Shepherd thrust his hands inside his black cloak. 'Murder? I know nothing of murder. We don't read newspapers. We keep ourselves apart.'

'Very Christian, I'm sure,' said Wexford. 'This girl came to your church. You knew her.'

'No.' The Shepherd shook his head vehemently. He looked angry and affronted. 'I have been away ill and someone else was in charge of my flock. Maybe she slipped in past him. Maybe, in his ignorance, he took her for one of the five hundred.'

'The five hundred?'

'Such is our number, the number of the elect on the face of the Earth. We make no converts. To be one of the Children you must be born to parents who are both Children, and thus the number swells and with death declines. Five hundred,' he said adding less loftily, 'give or take a little.' Gathering the heavy dull folds of his robe around him,' he muttered, 'I have work to do. Good day to you,' and marched off towards Queen's Lane.

Wexford made his way to the northern gate of the cemetery. The ground at this end was devoted to Catholic graves. A funeral had evidently taken place on the previous day and the flowers brought by mourners were wilting in the March wind. He took an unfamiliar path which led him between tombs whose occupants had been of the Greek Orthodox faith, and he noted an epitaph on a Russian princess. Her name and patronymic reminded him of Tolstoy's novels with their lists of *dramatis personae,* and he was trying to decipher the Cyrillic script when a shadow fell across the tomb and a voice said:

'Tatiana Alexandrovna Kratov.'

For the second time that day he had been surprised while

reading an inscription. Who was it now? Another churlish priest, bent on correcting him and reproving his ignorance? This time he turned round slowly to meet the eyes of a big man in a sheepskin jacket who stood, smiling cheerfully at him, his hands in his pockets.

'Do you know who she was?' Wexford asked, 'and how she came to be buried here?'

The man nodded. 'There's not much I don't know about this cemetery,' he said, 'or Kenbourne itself, for that matter.' A kind of boyish enthusiasm took the arrogance from his next words. 'I'm an expert on Kenbourne Vale, a walking mine of information.' He tapped the side of his head. 'There are unwritten history and geography books in here.'

'Then you must be . . .' What was the name Howard had given him? 'You're Notbourne Properties,' he said absurdly.

'The chairman.' Wexford's hand was taken in a strong grip. 'Stephen Dearborn. How do you do?'

7

*He thinketh himself so wise that he will not allow
another man's counsel.*

THEY had emerged into a windswept clearing, and now that
he examined him more closely, Wexford saw that his new
acquaintance was a man of substance. Dearborn's suit had
come from a price range to which Wexford could never aspire,
his shoes looked hand-made, and the strap of his watch was
a broad band of gold links.'

'You're a stranger here, are you?' Dearborn asked him.

'I'm on holiday.'

'And you thought you'd like to visit the scene of a recent
crime?'

Dearborn's voice was still friendly and pleasant, but Wexford thought he detected in it that note of distaste that was
sometimes present in his own when he spoke to ghoulish
sightseers. 'I know about the murder, of course,' he said, 'but
the cemetery is fascinating enough in itself.'

'You wouldn't agree with those people who are in favour
of deconsecrating the place and using it for building land?'

'I didn't know there was any such move on foot.' Wexford
saw that now the other man was frowning. 'You're opposed
to building?' he asked. 'To renovating the place?'

'Not at all,' Dearborn said energetically. 'I've been largely
responsible for improving Kenbourne Vale. I don't know how
much of the district you've seen, but the conversions in Cope-

land Square, for instance, they're my work. And the old Mont-fort house. My company's aim is to retrieve as much as possible of the Georgian and early Victorian from the wanton demolition that goes on. What I don't want to see is every place of interest like this cemetery levelled to make . . .' He spread out his arms and went on more hotly, '. . . character-less concrete jungles!'

'You live in Kenbourne Vale?' Wexford asked as to-gether they followed the path to St Peter's and the main gates.

'I was born here. I love every inch of the place, but I live in Chelsea. Laysbrook Place. Kenbourne Vale wouldn't suit my wife. It will one day when I've done with it. I want to make this the new Hampstead, the successor to fashionable Chelsea. And I can, I can!' Again Dearborn swept out an arm, strik-ing an ilex branch and sending dust-filled raindrops flying. 'I want to show people what's really here, hidden under the muck of a century, the beautiful façades, the grand squares. I'd show you over the cemetery now, only I don't suppose you've got the time and—well, it rather . . . I don't feel . . .'

'The murder,' said Wexford intuitively, 'has temporarily spoiled it for you?'

'In a way, yes. Yes, it has.' He gave Wexford a look of approval. 'Clever of you to guess that. You see, the odd thing is that that very girl came to me for a job. I interviewed her myself. Putting her body in that tomb seemed a sort of desecra-tion to me.' He shrugged. 'Let's not talk about it. What d'you think of this building, now?' he went on, pointing towards the sandstone dome. 'Eighteen-fifty-five and not a trace of the Gothic, but by then they had lost the art of emulating the Classical and were experimenting with Byzantine. Look at the length of those columns . . .' Laying a large hand on Wexford's arm, he plunged into a lecture on architectural styles, laced with obscure terms and words which to Wexford were almost meaningless. His listener's faint bewilderment com-municated itself to him and he stopped suddenly, saying, 'I'm boring you.'

'No, you're not. It's just that I'm afraid I'm rather ignorant. I find the district fascinating.'

'Do you?' The chairman of Notbourne Properties was evidently unused to an appreciative audience. 'I'll tell you what,' he said eagerly. 'Why don't you drop round and see us one night? Laysbrook House. I could show you maps of this place as it was a hundred and fifty years ago. I've got deeds of some of these old houses that would really interest you. What do you think?'

'I'd like that very much.'

'Let's see. It's Thursday now. Why not Saturday night? Come about half-past eight and we'll have a drink and go over the maps together. Now, can I give you a lift anywhere?'

But Wexford refused this invitation. The man had been kind and expansive to him. To confess now that he was a policeman, bound for Kenbourne Vale police station, might make Dearborn see him in the guise of a spy.

Instead of returning to the station, however, he turned eastwards along Lammas Grove in search of Sytansound. The police car parked outside told him where it was before he could read the shop sign. Sergeant Clements was at the wheel. He welcomed the chief inspector with a cheery, 'Had your lunch yet, sir?'

'I thought I might try your canteen,' Wexford said, getting in beside him. 'Would you recommend it?'

'I usually pop home if I can. I only live round the corner. I like to see the boy when I get the chance. He's in bed by the time I get home at night.'

'Your son?'

Clement's didn't reply at once. He was watching a boy unload something from a Sytansound van, but it seemed to Wexford that this was a simulated preoccupation, and he repeated his question. The sergeant turned back to face him. The strong colour in his cheeks had deepened to crimson and he cleared his throat.

'As a matter of fact,' he said, 'we're adopting him. We've

got him on three months probation, but the mother's signed the consent and we're due to get the order next week, a week tomorrow.' He slid his hands slowly around the wheel. 'If the mother changed her mind now I reckon it'd about kill my wife.'

Embarrassment and uncertainty had been transferred from one to the other, but there was nothing that Wexford could do about it now. 'Surely, if she's consented . . . ?'

'Well, sir, yes. That's what I keep telling my wife. We're ninety-nine per cent there. It's all been done through the proper channels, but natural mothers have been known to change their minds at the last minute and the court will always go with the mother even if she's given her consent in writing.'

'Do you know the mother?'

'No, sir. And she doesn't know us. We're just a serial number to her. It's done through what's called a guardian *ad litem,* she's a probation officer really. When the time comes the wife and I will go along to the court and the wife'll sit there with the boy on her lap—nice touch that, isn't it?—and the order'll be made and then—then he'll be ours for ever. Just as if he was our own.' Clements' voice grew thick and his lips trembled. 'But you can't help having just that one per cent chance in mind that something may go wrong.'

Wexford was beginning to feel sorry that he had ever opened the subject. The steering wheel which Clements' hands had gripped was wet with sweat and he could see a pulse drumming in his left temple. When he had spoken those last words he had looked near to actual tears.

'I take it Mr Fortune's inside the shop?' he said in an effort to change the subject. 'Who's the boy with the van?'

'That's Brian Gregson, sir. You've heard of him, I daresay. The one with the good friends all burning to give him an alibi.' Clements was calmer now as his attention was diverted from his personal problems back to the case. 'He's one of Sytansound's engineers, the only young unmarried one.'

Wexford remembered now that Howard had mentioned Gregson, but only in passing and not by name. 'What's this about an alibi?' he asked. 'And why should he need one?'

'He's just about the only man who ever associated with Loveday Morgan so-called. Tripper—that's the cemetery bloke—saw him giving her a lift home one night in his van. And one of the reps says Gregson used to chat her up in the shop sometimes.'

'A bit thin, isn't it?' Wexford objected.

'Well, his alibi for that Friday night is thin, too, sir. He *says* he was in the Psyche Club in Notting Hill—that's a sort of drinking place, sir. God knows what else goes on there—and four villains say he was with them there from seven till eleven. But three of them have got form. You couldn't trust them an inch. Look at him, sir. Wouldn't you reckon he'd got something to hide?'

He was a slight fair youth who seemed younger than the twenty-one years Howard had attributed to him and whose thin schoolboy arms looked too frail to support the boxes he was carrying from the van into the shop. Wexford thought he had the air of someone who believes that if he bustles away at his job, giving the impression of a rapt involvement, he may pass unnoticed and escape the interference of authority. Whether or not this was the hope that spurred him to trot in and out so busily with his loads, his work was destined to be interrupted. As he again approached the rear of the van, determindedly keeping his eyes from wandering towards the police car, a ginger-headed, sharp-faced man came out of Sytansound, beckoned to him and called out:

'Gregson! Here a minute!'

'That's Inspector Baker, sir,' said Clements. 'He'll put him through the mill all right, tell him a thing or two like his father should have done years ago.'

Wexford sighed to himself, for he sensed what was coming and knew that, short of getting out of the car, he was powerless to stop it.

'Vicious, like all the young today,' said Clements. 'Take these girls that have illegits, they've got no more idea of their responsibilities than—than rabbits.' He brought this last word out on a note of triumphant serendipity, perhaps believing that the chief inspector with his rustic background would be familiar with the behaviour of small mammals.

'They can't look after them,' he went on. 'You should have seen our boy when he first came to us, thin, white, his nose always running. I don't believe he'd been out in the fresh air since he was born. It isn't fair!' Clements' voice rose passionately. 'They don't want them, they'd have abortions only they leave it too late, while a decent, clean-living woman, a religious woman, like my wife has miscarriage after miscarriage and eats her heart out for years. I'd jail the lot of them, I'd...'

'Come now, Sergeant...' Wexford hardly knew what to say to calm him. He sought about in his mind for consoling platitudes, but before he could utter a single one the car door had opened and Howard was introducing him to Inspector Baker.

It was apparent from the moment that they sat down in the Grand Duke that Inspector Baker was one of those men who, like certain eager philosophers and scientists, form a theory and then force the facts to fit it. Anything which disturbs the pattern, however relevant, must be rejected, while insignificant data are grossly magnified. Wexford reflected on this in silence, saying nothing, for the inspector's conclusions had not been addressed to him. After the obligatory handshake and the mutterings of a few insincere words, Baker had done his best to exclude him from the discussion, adroitly managing to seat him at the foot of their table while he and Howard faced each other at the opposite end.

Clearly Gregson was Baker's candidate for the Morgan murder, an assumption he based on the man's record—a single conviction for robbery—the man's friends, and what he called the man's friendship with Loveday.

'He hung around her in the shop, sir. He gave her lifts in that van of his.'

'We know he gave her *a* lift,' said Howard.

66

Baker had a harsh unpleasant voice, the bad grammar of his childhood's cockney all vanished now, but the intonation remaining. He made everything he said sound bitter. 'We can't expect to find witnesses to every time they were together. They were the only young people in that shop. You can't tell me a girl like Morgan wouldn't have encouraged his attentions.'

Wexford looked down at his plate. He never liked to hear women referred to by their surnames without Christian name or style, not even when they were prostitutes, not even when they were criminals. Loveday had been neither. He glanced up as Howard said, 'What about the motive?'

Baker shrugged. 'Morgan encouraged him and then gave him the cold shoulder.'

Wexford hadn't meant to interrupt, but he couldn't help himself. 'In a *cemetery*?'

The inspector acted exactly like a Victorian parent whose discourse at the luncheon table had been interrupted by a child, one of those beings who were to be seen but not heard. But he looked as if he would have preferred not to see Wexford as well. He turned on him a reproving and penetrating stare, and asked him to repeat what he had said.

Wexford did so. 'Do people want to make love in cemeteries?'

For a moment it seemed as if Baker was going to do a Clements and say that 'they' would do anything anywhere. He appeared displeased by Wexford's mention of love-making, but he didn't refer to it directly. 'No doubt you have a better suggestion,' he said.

'Well, I have some questions,' Wexford said tentatively. 'I understand that the cemetery closes at six. What was Gregson doing all the afternoon?'

Howard, who seemed distressed by Baker's attitude, making up for it by a particularly delicate courtesy to his uncle, attending to his wants at the table and refilling his glass from the bottle of apple juice, said quickly, 'He was with Mrs Kirby in Copeland Road until about one-thirty, then back at Sytan-sound. After that he went to a house in Monmouth Street—

that's near Vale Park, Reg—and then he had a long repair job in Queen's Lane that took him until five-thirty, after which he went home to his parents' house in Shepherd's Bush.'

'Then I don't quite see . . .'

Baker had been crumbling a roll of bread into pellets with the air of a man preoccupied by his own thoughts. He raised his head and said in a way that is usually described as patient but in fact is a scarcely disguised exasperation, 'That the cemetery closes at six doesn't mean that no one can get in or out. There are breaches in the walls, quite a bad one at the end of Lammas Road, and vandals are always making them worse. The whole damned place ought to be ploughed up and built on.' Having given vent to his statement, utterly in opposition to Stephen Dearborn's views, he sipped his gin and gave a little cough. 'But that's by the way. You must admit, Mr Wexford, that you don't know this district like we do, and a morning's sightseeing isn't going to teach it to you.'

'Come, Michael,' Howard said uneasily. 'Mr. Wexford's anxious to learn. That's why he asked.'

Wexford was distressed to hear that his new acquaintance—his antagonist rather—shared Burden's Christian name. It reminded him bitterly how different his own inspector's response would have been. But he said nothing. Baker hardly seemed to have noticed Howard's mild reproof beyond giving a faint shrug. 'Gregson could have got in and out of the cemetery,' he said, 'as easily as you can swallow whatever that stuff is in your glass there.'

Wexford took a sip of the 'stuff' and tried again, determined not to let Howard see him show signs of offence. 'Have you a medical report yet?'

'We'll come to that in a minute. Gregson met her in Queen's Lane at half past five and they went to a secluded spot in the cemetery. She became frightened, screamed perhaps, and he strangled her to silence her.'

Why hadn't they gone to her room? Wexford asked himself. Why not to her room in that house where no questions were asked? And why had she taken the afternoon off if she didn't intend to meet Gregson until after work? These were questions he might ask Howard when they were alone together but not now. He saw that Baker was a man whose idea of a discussion was that he should be invited to state his views while the other so-called participants admired, agreed and encouraged him. Having given his own limited reconstruction of the case, he had turned to Howard once more and was attempting to discuss with him in an almost inaudible tone the findings of the medical report.

But Howard was determined not to exclude his uncle. Aware that Wexford had a small reputation as an investigator into quirks of character, he pressed Wexford to tell them about his morning's work.

'She was a very innocent girl,' Wexford began. He felt he was on safe ground here, for Baker could hardly claim to be as conversant with the personality of the dead girl as he was with the geography of Kenbourne Vale. 'She was very shy,' he said, 'afraid to go to parties, and very likely she'd only once in her life been into a public house.' He was pleased to see a smile of what might have been approval on Baker's face. It encouraged him to be bolder, to ask a question which might seem to reflect on the inspector's theory. 'Would a girl like that lead a man on, go alone with a comparative stranger into a lonely place? She'd be too frightened.'

Baker went on smiling tightly.

'There was another point that struck me . . .'

'Let's have it, Reg. It may be helpful.'

'Tuesday was February the 29th. I've been wondering if he put her in the Montfort vault because he knew it was only visited on the last Tuesday of the month and that Tuesday, he thought, had already gone by.'

Baker looked incredulous, but Howard's eyes narrowed. 'You mean he *forgot* that this year, Leap Year, there was an extra Tuesday in the month?'

'It's a possibility, isn't it? I don't think a boy like Gregson would know about the vault and the trust. I was thinking that the man who killed her did know and that he might have put her in there because Loveday knew something he didn't want revealed before a few weeks had passed by.'

'Interesting,' said Howard. 'How does that strike you, Michael?'

The man who was not Burden, who shared with Burden only a Christian name and a certain sharp-featured fairness, raised his eyebrows and drawled, 'To your—er, uncle's other point, sir?' It was clever the hesitation he managed before saying 'uncle's', just sufficiently emphasising the nepotism. But he had gone a little too far. His remark brought a frown to Howard's usually gentle face and set him tapping his fingers against his wineglass. And Baker understood that he was admonished. He shrugged, smiled and spoke with cool courtesy.

'You called Morgan innocent and shy, Mr Wexford, but I'm sure you know how deceptive appearances can be. Post-mortem findings, on the other hand, aren't deceptive. Would it surprise you to hear that, according to the medical report, she gave birth to a child during the past year?'

8

*Away they trudge, I say, out of their known and
accustomed houses, finding no place to rest in.*

AFTER Howard's kindness and the cheerful, matter-of-fact
welcome he had received from other members of Howard's force, Wexford felt Baker's antagonism almost painfully.
He was curiously disheartened. His first day here—his first day
anywhere, come to that—as a private investigator had begun
so promisingly. Baker's intervention had been like a dark
cloud putting out the sun.

He knew that if he had been fit and quite well, if his confidence hadn't been shaken by his tough old body suddenly
betraying him, he would have taken this small reverse in his
stride. He wasn't, after all, a child to be put off playing his
favourite game because another stronger and healthier child
had come along and tried to show him how the bricks ought to
be stacked. But now within himself he felt almost childlike, his
bold adult identity once more disturbed. And when he
looked back on his morning's work, it seemed amateurish. The
appalling thought that Howard had sent him off on a little
hunt of his own simply to occupy him and keep him happy
couldn't be resisted.

Nor was he much comforted by the private office which
Howard had set aside for his use and to which Detective
Constable Dinehart had just conducted him. Like all the rooms
Wexford had seen in this police station, it was dark, gloomy
and with an enormously high ceiling. This one had a bit of

greyish carpet, chairs covered in slippery brown leather, and the view from the window was a full frontal one of Kenbourne gasworks. He couldn't help thinking nostalgically of his own office in Kingsmarkham which was bright and modern, and, looking at the pitch pine, pitted monstrosity in front of him, of his beloved rosewood desk, damson-red and always laden with his own particular clutter.

Sitting down, he asked himself sharply what was the matter with him. Howard's house was too grand for him, this place too shabby. What did he expect? That London would be a Utopian Kingsmarkham and that all these London coppers were going to roll out the red carpet for him?

He stared at the gasometer, wondering how he was going to pass the afternoon. 'Poke about all you like,' Howard had said, but where was he to poke about and how much authority had he got? He was considering whether it would be pushing or against protocol for him to seek Howard out when his nephew tapped on the door and came in.

Howard looked tired. His was a face which easily showed wear and tear. The grey eyes had lost their brightness and the skin under them was puffy.

'How d'you like your office?'

'It's fine, thanks.'

'Horrible outlook, I'm afraid, but it's either that or the brewery or the bus station. I want to apologise for Baker.'

'Come off it, Howard,' said Wexford.

'No. His treatment of you was rude but not indefensible. One has to make allowances for Baker. He's been under a good deal of strain lately. He married a girl half his age. She became pregnant, which made him very happy until she told him the child was another man's and she was leaving him for that other man. Since then he's lost his confidence, distrusts people and is chronically afraid of not being up to the job.'

'I see. It's a nasty story.'

They were both silent for a moment. Wexford found himself hoping desperately that Howard wouldn't go away again, leaving him alone with the gasworks and his depressing thoughts. To keep him there a little longer, he said, 'About this child of Loveday Morgan's . . .'

'That's really why I came to talk to you,' Howard said. 'I don't know what to think. I don't even know if it's significant in this case, and I need to talk it over with someone. With you.'

Wexford felt himself relax with relief. His nephew sounded sincere. Perhaps, after all . . . 'The child may be with his or her grandparents,' he said, and as he spoke he felt the case beginning to drive self-pitying thoughts from his mind. 'You've still heard nothing of them?'

'We're doing everything possible to trace them. For one thing, they'll have to be found before she can be buried, but I'm beginning to think they must be dead. Oh, I know that these days girls are always having differences with their parents and leaving home, but often that only makes the parents more anxious about them. What sort of people who have a missing, or at least absent, blonde twenty-year-old daughter, could read all the newspaper stories there have been these past few days and not get in touch with us?'

'Very simple unimaginative people, perhaps, Howard. Or people who just don't connect their daughter with Loveday Morgan because that isn't her real name and they don't know that their daughter was living in Kenbourne Vale.'

Howard shrugged. 'It's as if she dropped out of the blue, Reg, arrived in Kenbourne Vale two months ago without a history. Let me put you a bit more fully into the picture. Now, as you know, although we don't have absolute cards of identity as certain European nationals do, everyone has a medical card and a National Insurance number. There was no medical card in Loveday Morgan's room and she was on none of the local doctor's lists. It's inconceivable that she should have been the private patient of any doctor, but maybe she was so healthy that she didn't need medical attention. But she had a *child*, Reg. Where? Who attended her at the birth?

'When she first went to Sytansound, Gold asked her for her National Insurance card. She told him she hadn't got one and

73

he sent her along to the Social Security people to get a card which she did in the name of Loveday Morgan.'

'Stop a minute, Howard,' said his uncle. 'That means that she had never worked before. A working-class girl of twenty who had never worked . . .'

'She may, of course, have worked before and had a card in her real name. They don't ask for your birth certificate, you know, only your name and where you were born and so on. I really don't think there's anything to stop anyone from getting half a dozen cards and fraudulently claiming sickness benefit and unemployment money, only that one day they'd catch up with you. Of couse, there are certain jobs you can do where you needn't have a card at all. Most charwomen don't. Prostitutes don't. Nor do those who make their living by crime or drug pushing. But surely Loveday Morgan wasn't any of those things?'

Wexford shook his head. 'She seems the last girl in the world who would have had an illegitimate child.'

'You know what they say, it's the good girls who have the babies. Now, as well as her parents, we're trying to trace her child. It isn't fostered in Kenbourne Vale, we've established that. It could be anywhere. D'you know what I find hardest of all to understand, Reg?'

Wexford looked enquiring.

'I can see that she might have had reasons for wanting to cover her tracks, for wanting to be anonymous. She may, for instance, have had possessive parents who tried to deny her a life of her own. She may have been hiding from some man who threatened her—a point that, I must remember that. But what I can't fathom at all is why she had apparently been *doing this for years*. It almost looks as if years ago she avoided going to a doctor or getting a National Insurance card so that one day, *now*, when she came to die by violence, she would appear to have had a life of no more than two months duration, to have dropped from another planet.'

'What about this Fulham address?' Wexford asked.

'The one she gave Peggy Pope? It's a house in Belgrade

74

Road, as I told you, but she was never there.'

'The owners of the house ... ?'

'I suppose they could be lying, playing some deep game of their own, but all the neighbours aren't. I expect Loveday went along Belgrade Road in a bus one day and the name stuck in her mind. I realise, of course, that when you give a false address, unless you simply make up a name, the address you give is that of a street you've either seen or heard of in some connection that causes it to remain in your memory. But the mind is so complex, Reg, and she isn't alive to be psychoanalysed. If she were, we wouldn't be doing this, talking this way.'

'I was thinking that she might have known someone in this Belgrade Road.'

'You mean we ought to do a house to house on the chance of that?'

'Well, *I* could,' said Wexford.

He weighed himself before he went to bed and found that he had lost five pounds. But instead of being cheered by this in the morning he awoke depressed. It was raining. Like a humble trainee, he was going to have to plod round Fulham in the rain. And where, anyway, *was* Fulham?

Denise had stuck a rather alarming flower arrangement on the landing, a confection which was to floral decoration as Dali is to painting. A branch of holly grabbed him as he started to go downstairs and when he freed himself his hand came into disagreeable contact with a spider plant.

'Where's Fulham?' he asked as he ate his sugarless grapefruit. 'Not miles away I hope.'

Denise said, 'It's just down the road.' She added mournfully, 'Some people call *this* Fulham.'

She didn't ask why he wanted to know. She and Dora thought he was going for his favourite Embankment walk, not understanding that he hated the river when it was shivering and prickly with rain. By now it was falling steadily, not country rain which washes and freshens and brings with it a green scent, but London rain, dirty and soot-smelling. He went westwards, crossed Stamford Bridge and past the gates to the football ground. By the station, fans were buying Chelsea scarves and badges in the sports souvenir shops. Young couples stared disconsolately at secondhand furniture, battered three-piece suites growing damp on the pavement. In North End Road traffic crawled between the stalls, splashing shoppers. But it was more the sort of thing he was used to, a bit like Stowerton really. Here was none of the jaded and somehow sinister sophistication of Kenbourne Vale. The side streets looked suburban. They had gardens and whole families lived in them. Housewives shopped here with proper shopping baskets and almost everyone he passed seemed to belong to an order of society with which he was familiar.

He laughed at himself for being like a conventional old fuddy-duddy, and then he saw Belgrade Road ahead of him, debouching at a right angle from the main street. The houses were three storeys tall, sixty or seventy years old, terraced. At the end, as in Garmisch Terrace, was a church, but grey and spired and as a church should be. He furled the umbrella he was carrying and began on his house to house.

There were a hundred and two houses in Belgrade Road. He went first to the one where Loveday said she had lived, a cared-for house which had recently been painted. Even the brickwork had been painted, and it was a curious colour to choose for an English house in a grimy street, a bright rose-pink. Number seventy. It had a name too, Rosebank, printed in white on pink, the sign swinging in the rain. Had she chosen it for the number? For the name? Had she even seen it?

A couple lived there, Howard had said, and it was a young woman who answered his ring. It made him feel rather awkward asking about a girl with fair hair, quiet and reserved, a girl who might have had a baby with her, for this woman was also a blonde and she carried a young child supported on her hip.

'They came and asked me before,' she said. 'I told them we never let rooms or a flat.' She added proudly, 'We live in the *whole* house.'

76

He tried the immediate neighbours, worked back to the main street from which this one turned, then up towards the church, down the other side. A lot of people in Belgrade Road let rooms and he talked to half a dozen landladies who sent him off to other landladies. At one point he thought he was getting somewhere. A West Indian hospital orderly who worked nights but showed no dismay at being awakened from his sleep, remembered young Mrs Maitland who had lived on the top floor of number 59 and whose husband had abandoned her and her baby in December. She had moved away a couple of weeks later.

Wexford went back to 59 where he had previously met with ungraciousness on the part of the owner, and met this time with pugnacity. 'I told you my daughter was living here. How many more times, I should like to know? Will you go away and let me get on with my cooking? She left in December and she's living up Shepherd's Bush way. I saw her last night and she wasn't dead then. Does that satisfy you?'

Disheartened, he went on. There was no point in giving her name. He was sure she hadn't called herself Loveday Morgan until she went to live in Garmisch Terrace. All he could do was repeat the description and enquire about anyone known to have moved away at the end of the previous year. The rain fell more heavily. What a stupid invention an umbrella was, almost useless for a job like this! But he put it up again, tilting it backwards while he stood under the dripping porches.

Facing the rose-pink house and on the corner of the only side street to run out of Belgrade Road was a little shop, a general store, very like those to be found in the villages near Kingsmarkham. Wexford marvelled to see such a place here, only a hundred yards from a big shopping centre, and marvelled still more to see that it was doing a thriving trade. There was just one assistant serving the queue, a shabby little woman with a mole on the side of her nose, and he made his enquiries of her briefly, anxious not to keep her from her work. She had a curious flat voice, free from cockney, and she was patient with him, but neither she nor the woman shopper behind him

—a resident of the side street—could recall anyone answering his description who had moved away in December.

About twenty houses remained to be visited. He visited them all, feeling very cold now and wondering how he was going to explain to Dora that he had got soaked to the skin. Between them all they were turning him into a hypochondriac, he thought, and he began to feel nervous, asking himself what all this tramping about and getting wet might be doing to his health. Crocker would have a fit if he could see him now, water running from his hair down the back of his neck as he emerged from the last house. Well, Crocker didn't know everything, and for the rest of the day and all tomorrow until the evening he would take it easy.

He paused and, turning back, surveyed the whole length of the street once more. Through the falling silvery rain, under the massy clouds which were streaming across the sky from behind the grey church spire, Belgrade Road looked utterly commonplace. Nothing but the church and the pink house distinguished it from a sister street which ran from the main highway in the opposite direction, and this latter was, if anything, more interesting and memorable. Buses used it and on a sunny day both sides of it would catch the full sun for hours. Why, then had Loveday Morgan chosen Belgrade Road?

He tried to imagine himself giving a false address in London. What street would *he* choose? Not one that he had stayed in or knew well, for that might lead to discovery. Say Lammas Grove, West Fifteen? Number 43, for instance. Immediately he asked himself why, and reasoned that he had picked the street because he had sat outside Sytansound there with Sergeant Clements, the number was just a number that had come to him. . . .

So that was how it was done. That was the way Howard had inferred that it was done, and he had been right again. Obviously, then, it was hopeless to try to trace Loveday by these means. He must approach the matter from other angles.

9

In them they have . . . all manner of fruit, herbs and
flowers, so pleasant, so well furnished, and so finely
kept, that I never saw thing more fruitful nor better
trimmed in any place.

GOING out in the evening was one of the excesses on
which Crocker had placed a strict ban. If Wexford's
faith in the doctor had been shaken, his wife's had not. She
could only be consoled by his promise to take a taxi to Laysbrook Place, to abstain from strong drink and not to stay out
too long.

He was looking forward to this visit. A little judicious
questioning might elicit from Dearborn more information
about the cemetery. Was it, for instance, as easy to get in and
out after the gates were closed as Baker had insisted? Before
Tripper and his fellows went home at night did they make
any sort of search of the place? Or must Loveday have been
killed before six? If this was so, Gregson, occupied at work,
would be exonerated. And might Dearborn not also know
something of Loveday herself? He had interviewed her. It was
possible that, at that interview, she had told him something
of her past history.

Laysbrook Place was one of those country corners of
London in which the air smells sweeter, birds sometimes sing
and other trees grow apart from planes. An arch, hung with
a brown creeper Wexford thought was wistaria, concealed most
of the little street from Laysbrook Square. He walked under
it, light falling about him from two lamps on brackets, and

saw ahead of him a single house such as might have stood in Kingsmarkham High Street. It wasn't an old house but old bricks and timber had been used in its construction, and it was like no London house Wexford had seen. For one thing, it was rather low and sprawling with gables and lattice windows; for another, it had a real garden with apple trees in it and shrubs that were probably lilac. Now, in early March, forsythia blazed yellow and luminous through the lamplit dark and, as he opened the gate, he saw snowdrops in drifts as thick and white as real snow.

The front door opened before he reached it and Stephen Dearborn came down the steps.

'What a lovely place,' Wexford said.

'You'd agree with my wife, then, that it's an improvement on Kenbourne?'

Wexford smiled, sighing a little to himself, for he had been so piercingly reminded of the country. He was suddenly conscious of the peace and the silence. Not even in Howard's house had he been able to escape from the ceaseless sound of traffic, but there was nothing more to be heard than a faint throbbing, what Londoners call the 'hum', ever present in the city and its suburbs but sometimes so remote as to seem like a sound in one's own head.

'My wife's upstairs with our daughter,' Dearborn said. 'She wouldn't go to sleep and it's no good my staying with her. I just want to cuddle her and play with her all the time.'

It was warm inside but airy, enough heat turned on to take off the March chill without making one gasp. The house was very obviously the residence of a rich man, but Wexford couldn't see any sign of pretentiousness or evidence that money had been spent with an eye to impress. It wasn't even very tidy. There was a scattering of crumbs under a tea-table and an ivory teething ring lay on a blanket in the middle of the carpet.

'What will you drink?'

Wexford was getting tired of drawing attention to his illness and his diet. 'Have you any beer?' he asked.

'Sure we have. I couldn't get through the weekend without it after all those shorts I have to consume the rest of the time. I drink it from the can, as a matter of fact.' Dearborn gave a sudden boyish smile. 'We'd better have glasses or my wife will kill me after you've gone.'

The beer was kept in a refrigerator with a wood veneered door which Wexford had at first glance taken for a glass cabinet. 'My favourite toy,' said Dearborn. 'When Alexandra gets a bit older I shall always keep it full of ice cream and cans of coke.' Still smiling, he filled their glasses. 'I've come to fatherhood rather late in life, Mr Wexford—I was forty-three last Tuesday—and my wife says it's made me soppy. I'd like to get the moon and stars for my daughter, but, as this is impossible, she shall have all the good things of this world instead.'

'You're not afraid of spoiling her?'

'I'm afraid of many things, Mr Wexford.' The smile died away and he became intensely serious. 'Of being too indulgent and too possessive among other things. I tell myself that she's not mine, that she belongs to herself. It's not easy being a parent.'

'No, it's not easy. And it's as well people don't know it, for if they did, maybe they wouldn't dare have children.'

Dearborn shook his head. 'I could never feel like that. I'm a fortunate man. I've been lucky in marriage. And you know what they say, happy is the man who can make a living from his hobby. But, for all that, I didn't know what real happiness was till I got Alexandra. If I lost her I'd—I'd kill myself.'

'Oh, come, you mustn't say that.'

'It's true. I mean it. You don't believe me?'

But Wexford, who had many times heard men make similar threats without taking them very seriously, did believe him. There was a kind of earnest desperation in the man's whole manner, and he was relieved when the tension was slackened by the entry of Mrs Dearborn.

She told him she was glad to see him. 'As long as you don't

encourage Stephen to cart us all off to some slum,' she said. 'He gets tired of places he can't improve.'

'It would be hard to improve on Laysbrook House,' said Wexford politely.

She was not at all beautiful and she had made no attempt to look younger than her forty years. Her walnut-brown hair was threaded with grey, her neck ringed with lines. He wondered what constituted her appeal. Was it the willowy ease with which she moved—for she was very slim—or the play of her long fine hands or her extreme femininity? The last, he thought. Her nails were varnished, her skirt short, she was even now taking a cigarette from a cedarwood box, but for all that she had all the old-fashioned womanly grace of a lady out of one of Trollope's novels, a squire's lady, a chatelaine.

That Dearborn was in love with her was immediately apparent from the way his eyes followed her to her chair and lingered on her, watching her settle herself and smooth her skirt over her crossed legs. It was almost as if those briefly caressing hands had for a moment become his own and, vicariously, he felt under them the smoothness of silk and flesh.

Wexford was wondering how to broach the subject of Kenbourne cemetery when Dearborn announced that it was time to get the maps out.

'Dull for you, darling,' he said. 'You've heard it all so many times before.'

'I can bear it. I shall knit.'

'Yes, do. I like to see you knitting. It's a funny thing, Mr Wexford, the qualities women think will attract us and the qualities which really do. I could watch Miss World doing a striptease and it would leave me cold, but let me see a woman in a clean white apron rolling pastry and I'd be in love with her before she could close the kitchen door.'

Mrs Dearborn laughed. 'That's true,' she said. 'You were.'

So that's the way they came together, Wexford thought. It really happened and not too long ago either. It must have been like a Dutch interior, the man visiting the house as a guest for the first time, the kitchen door half open and behind it this brown-haired woman with the sweet face looking up, startled from her cooking, shy at being caught in her apron and with flour on her arms.

Mrs Dearborn seemed to sense what was going on in his mind, for her eyes met his fleetingly and she pursed her lips, suppressing a smile. Then she lifted from a bag a mass of wool and half-completed work, as white and fluffy as flour, and began to knit.

To watch her was curiously soothing. Every harassed businessman, he thought, should have a tank of tropical fish at one end of his office and a woman knitting at the other. Tired now, he could have watched her all the evening, but he had to turn his attention to the maps, photographs and the old deeds which Dearborn had brought into the room and spread in front of them.

The enthusiasm of the crusader had taken hold of Dearborn and as he talked a light came into his eyes. This was Kenbourne as it had been in the time of the fourth George; here had stood the manor house which a royal duke had rented for his actress mistress; on the south side of Lammas Grove had stood a row of magnificent elms. Why shouldn't the land be cleared and fresh trees planted? Why not make all this waste stretch here into playing fields? There was no need for Wexford to ask about the cemetery. Before he could interrupt he was told its acreage, the history of every interesting person buried there, and informed that the state of the walls on the eastern side was so bad that soon vandals would be able to enter and plunder at will.

A point to Baker. Wexford tried to relax and make himself receptive, but he felt overwhelmed. He was experiencing a sensation he had often had before when lectured by someone with an obsession. It is all too much. It should be done in easy stages, but the obsessed cannot see this. Night and day he has lived with his passion and when he comes to enlighten the tyro, he is unable, because he has not been trained in teaching, to sketch in a simple background, awaken interest and postpone the complex details until another occasion. Unrelated facts, historical anecdotes, instances of iconoclasm came tumbling from Dearborn's lips. He found maps to confirm this, deeds to verify that, until Wexford's head began to spin.

It was a relief when the time came for his glass to be refilled and he could lean back briefly to exchange a smile with Mrs Dearborn. But when he looked in her direction, expecting to be calmed by the sight of those rhythmically moving fingers, he saw that her work lay in her lap, her eyes were fixed in a dead stare on a distant part of the room, and she was compulsively picking at the piping on the arm of her chair.

The piping had been so badly frayed that the cord beneath was fully exposed on both arms. This was not the result of one evening of nervous tension but surely of many. And when he glanced at the other five or six chairs in the room and at the sofa, he saw that all, though otherwise immaculate, were in the same state. Loops of cord showed on every arm, protruding from feathery rags.

The sight upset him, for it seemed to destroy the picture he had of this couple's serene happiness. He felt a sudden tension. At the drinks tray Dearborn stood watching his wife, his face compassionate yet very slightly exasperated.

No one spoke. Into the silence the telephone rang shatteringly, making them jump but none of them as violently as Mrs Dearborn. She was out of her chair on the second ring, her sharp 'I'll get it!' almost a cry. Her grace had gone. She was like a medium who, awakened from a strange and transcending communion, must gather together the threads that hold her to reality and, in gathering them, suffers intolerable mental stress.

The telephone was at the far end of the room, on a table under the point on which Mrs Dearborn's eyes had long been fixed. She took the receiver and said hallo, clearing her throat so that she could repeat the word in a voice above a whisper. That she wanted the call and was not afraid of it was apparent; that the wrong person had called showed in the sudden sagging of her shoulders.

'That's all right,' she said into the mouthpiece, and then to her husband, 'Only a wrong number.'

'We get so many,' Dearborn said, as if apologising for a fault of his own. 'You're tired, Melanie. Let me give you a drink.'

'Yes,' she said. 'Yes, thanks.' She pushed a lock of hair from her forehead and Wexford saw how thin her wrists were. 'It's my daughter,' she said, the good hostess who knows that there must be no subterfuge before guests. 'I get so worried about her. Children are an anxiety these days, aren't they? You never know what trouble they may be in. But I won't bore you.' She took the whisky her husband handed her. 'Thank you, darling.' She sighed.

Husband and wife stood facing each other, hands briefly locked. Wexford was even more in the dark than before. What had she meant about her daughter, about not knowing what trouble she might be in? A baby young enough to use a teething ring, a baby its mother had left upstairs an hour before, was surely peacefully sleeping in its cot. Unless she was expecting a doctor to phone her because the child had been ill . . .

He drank his second glass of beer with a feeling of guilt. The unfamiliar alcohol made him feel lethargic and light-headed and he was glad when Dearborn packed up his papers and said that was enough for one night.

'You must come again. Or, better than that, I'll take you on a tour round some of the places we've talked about. I take Alexandra to Kenbourne Vale.' He spoke quite seriously. 'She's not really old enough yet to understand, but you can see in her eyes she's beginning to take an interest. She's a very intelligent child. Are you in London for long?'

'Only till next Saturday, I'm afraid. Then it's back to Sussex and work.'

'What sort of work?' Mrs Dearborn asked.

'I'm a policeman.'

'How interesting. Not an ordinary policeman, I'm sure.'

'A detective chief inspector.'

Her face sharpened. She looked at her husband, then away. Dearborn might have been expected to refer to the murder, but he didn't. 'That puts paid to our tour,' he said. 'You're going home and I've got an architect's convention in Yorkshire at the end of next week. Next time you come to London, maybe?'

Wexford nodded, but all further conversation was cut short by a wailing cry from upstairs. The adored, troublesome, precocious, super-intelligent infant was once more awake.

Melanie Dearborn, who had been so electrified by the telephone bell, behaved now like a woman who had reared six children. With a 'That's Alexandra off again,' she rose casually from her chair. It was Dearborn who made the fuss. Was the child ill? Should they call a doctor? He hadn't liked the rash on her face, although his wife had said it was only teething.

Wexford took advantage of this small crisis to leave them, furnishing them with Howard's telephone number and thanking them for a pleasant evening. Mrs Dearborn saw him out. Her husband was already upstairs, calling to the baby that Daddy was coming, that Daddy would make everything all right.

10

For as love is oftentimes won with beauty, so it is not kept, preserved and continued but by virtue and obedience.

WHILE Wexford was with the Dearborns and Howard at home playing bridge a burglary took place in Kenbourne Vale. It was one of a series, all break-ins involving the theft of silver or jewellery and cash and all occurring on Friday or Saturday nights.

'Your friend's answerable for some of this,' said Howard on Monday morning.'

'Dearborn?' Wexford queried.

'Kenbourne's coming up, you see, Reg. I'm all for improving the place, converting some of these old slums and so on, but there's no doubt that when you bring money in you bring crime too. Ten years ago there was scarcely a Kenbournite, excepting the shopkeepers, with anything worth pinching. Now, in the better parts, we've got company directors with heirlooms and safes a child could open. None of the break-ins have been in places owned by Notbourne Properties yet, but unless I'm much mistaken they'll go for Vale Park next.'

'Any idea who "they" are?'

'One always has. You know that,' Howard said bitterly. 'I spent most of yesterday questioning a man called Winter who has, of course, a beautiful unbreakable alibi. And who do you think is supplying it for him? None other than our old friend Harry Slade.'

Wexford looked puzzled. 'Not an old friend of mine.'

'Sorry, Reg. Haven't we put you in the picture? Harry Slade is one of the men who says Gregson was with him in the Psyche Club on the night of Friday, February 25th. He hasn't got a record but I'm beginning to think he's a professional alibi provider.'

'But surely . . . ?'

'Surely his word counts for nothing? Not to a judge, Reg. Here's a blameless citizen, a milkman of all things, pure as the goods he purveys, who says Winter spent Saturday night with himself, his dear old mother and his typist fiancée, playing Monopoly—again of all things—in mother's flat.'

'At least it gives you another lever against Gregson,' Wexford said as Baker entered the room. He spoke placatingly, for he pitied any man who feared he was losing his grip, but Baker eyed him with frosty politeness. He had the face of a cheetah, Wexford thought, all nose and little sharp mouth, the forehead receding and the gingery hair growing down his cheeks in sideburns.

'If you're going to Sytansound now, Michael,' said Howard, 'you might take my uncle with you.'

'Nothing would please me more, sir,' said Baker, 'but I'm taking Sergeant Nolan as it is, and I've promised to show young Dinehart the ropes. Won't it be rather using a sledgehammer to swat a fly?'

Wexford found it hard to keep his temper, to smile and pretend for Howard's benefit that he was happy to be the onlooker who is said to see most of the game. He reminded himself of Baker's unhappy history, the cruel young wife and the child who was not his. *Tout comprendre, c'est tout pardonner.* But what was he going to do with himself for the rest of the day? Gossip with Howard and distract him from his work? Potter about Kenbourne? He was beginning to understand just what Howard's kind act of opting him on to his force in an honorary capacity amounted to. He did no harm, he appeared to amuse himself, he supplied ideas for experts to demolish; he was like, he thought, a workman whose usefulness is at end, who should really be made redundant, but for whom a kindly boss finds a job which could more efficiently be done by a computer if it even needed to be done at all.

He might as well go home and take Dora to the pictures. In the entrance hall he met Sergeant Clements.

'Have a good weekend, sir?'

'Very pleasant, thank you. How's that boy of yours?'

'He's grand, sir. Had the wife up in the night, the little beggar, yelling his head off, but when she went in to him all he wanted was to play. The way he laughs! He's starting to crawl. He'll walk before he's a year old.'

These fathers! 'What are you going to call him?'

'Well, sir, I think his mother must have been one of the romantic kind, fond of fancy names. She called him Barnabas, but the wife and I, we like something plainer, so we've settled for James after my old dad. As soon as we've got that adoption order out of the way we'll have a proper christening.'

'Only four days to go, isn't it?'

Clements nodded. His cheerfulness had suddenly evaporated at the reminder of the short time—the agonisingly short, agonisingly long time—which separated probationary father-hood from the real thing. Or denied him fatherhood alto-gether? Looking at the man's red weathered face which, for all his vaunted worldly wisdom, remained immature and schoolboyish, Wexford thought of the coming Friday with a small shiver of dread. Suppose this young woman, this roman-tic girl who had named her child fancifully, changed her mind again and came into the court to claim him? What would life be like then for Clements and his good patient wife, alone and desolate on top of their tower? It was fine and just, this law which gave prime consideration to the natural mother and her child, but it was a cruel law for the sterile who waited and longed and prayed.

'You've shown such an interest in our boy, sir,' Clements

said, smiling again, 'that the wife and I were wondering if you'd come along one day and have a bite of lunch with us and—well, see young James. Say tomorrow or Wednesday? We'd take it as an honour.'

Wexford was touched. 'Tomorrow will be fine,' he said, reflecting that it would be a way of passing the time. On an impulse, he patted the sergeant's shoulder.

Denise and Dora had just finished their lunch. Neither expressed surprise at seeing him or shock that he was still alive. There was a look in his wife's eyes that he had not seen there for many years.

'What have you been up to, Uncle Reg?' asked Denise, for the first time in their acquaintance cyeing him as a man rather than as an ancient invalid.

'Me?' said Wexford ungrammatically. 'What d'you mean?' It was odd, he thought, how guilty the innocent can be made to feel. Certainly the telegram: Fly at once, all is discovered, would send half the population packing their bags and making for the nearest airport. 'What d'you mean, "up to"?'

'Well, a woman's been phoning for you, a Melanie something. I didn't catch the last name. She said, could you go round and see her and in the daytime, please, *when her husband is out*. You're to phone her back and she says you know the number.'

Wexford was puzzled, but he burst out laughing just the same.

'Who is she, Reg?' said Dora, not quite believing she was deceived, but not entirely happy either.

'Melanie?' he said airily. 'Oh, *Melanie* Just a woman I'm having a red-hot affair with. You know all those times you thought I was over at Kenbourne with Howard? Well, actually I was with her. There's many a good tune played on an old fiddle, my dear.' He stopped, caught his wife's eye. It was admonitory, yet faintly distressed. 'Dora!' he said. 'Look at me. Look at *me*. What woman in her right mind would want *me*?'

'I would.'

'Oh, *you*.' He was oddly moved. He kissed her lightly. 'That's the blindness of love,' he said. 'Excuse me. I'll just give my mistress a tinkle.'

Dearborn was in the phone book, Stephen T., with some letters after it that Wexford thought indicated architectural qualifications. He dialled and Melanie Dearborn answered on the second ring. Did she always? Had she been sitting by the phone to jump out of her skin when it rang?

'I'm very sorry to trouble you Mr Wexford. I—I . . . Would it be a great imposition to ask you if you could come over here and see me?'

'Now, Mrs Dearborn?'

'Well, yes, please. Now.'

'Can you give me some idea what it's about?'

'May I leave that until I see you?'

Much intrigued, Wexford said, 'Give me ten minutes,' and rang off. He explained to Denise and Dora, or rather gave them what explanation he could, for he had no more idea than they as to why Melanie Dearborn wanted to see him in her husband's absence. Could it be that she was genuinely worried about Dearborn's obsession with the transformation of Kenbourne Vale because his passion led him to neglect her or his business? Or was it anxiety over some aspect of Alexandra's welfare that distressed her? Neither of these answers seemed probable.

'The library have got your book in, Uncle Reg,' said Denise. 'You can call in for it on your way back.'

As he picked up the blue card and left the house, he came to the conclusion that Mrs Dearborn had sent for him because he was a policeman.

The cab came to a halt at a double white line, and on the major road a red Mini passed them, coming from the direction of Laysbrook Square. Wexford caught only a quick glimpse of its driver, a young woman in a dark coat. Her gloved hands rang a bell in his mind but summoned nothing from its recesses, and he forgot the gloved girl when the taxi brought him under the mews arch and he saw Melanie Dearborn waiting for him on the steps of Laysbrook House.

Wexford achieved a calm and, he hoped, reassuring smile for her, but she did not smile back. She clasped his hand in both hers and began to let forth a stream of apologies for disturbing someone who was only a slight acquaintance.

His guess had been right. 'It's because you're a policeman,' she said when they were inside. 'Or rather, because you're a detective, but not exactly working at the moment, if you know what I mean.'

Wexford didn't.

'You can tell me what I ought to do,' she said, dropping into a chair and immediately applying both hands to the piping cords.

'I'm not so sure of that,' he demurred. She was such a nice woman and so obviously distressed that he allowed himself advice that should only have come from an intimate friend. 'Try to relax,' he said. 'Your hands . . . Let me give you a cigarette.'

She nodded, pulling her hands away from the chair arms and clutching one in the other. 'You're a soothing sort of person, aren't you?' she said as he lit her cigarette. 'I feel a bit better.'

'That's good. What's it all about?'

'My daughter,' said Melanie Dearborn. 'She's missing. I don't know where she is. Ought I to report her as a missing person?'

Wexford stared. 'The *baby*? You mean someone has taken the *baby*?'

'Oh, no, no, of course not! Alexandra is upstairs. I mean my elder daughter, Louise. She's twenty-one.' It was pathetic the way she waited shyly for the gallant thing to be said. Wexford couldn't say it. Today Mrs Dearborn looked amply old enough to be the mother of a grown-up daughter. But Dearborn—was he the father? He could have sworn this pair hadn't been married more than three or four years. 'She's not Stephen's,' said Mrs Dearborn. 'I was married before. I was only nineteen when Louise was born and my first husband died when she was ten.'

'What makes you think she's missing? Does she usually live here?'

'No. She never has. She and Stephen don't get on, but I don't really know why not. They used to and it was actually through Isa—she calls herself that—that I first met Stephen. I suppose she resented my marrying again.'

An old story. The mother and daughter close, the interloping lover who leaves the daughter out in the cold.

'We got married three years ago,' she said. 'Isa was still at school, waiting to do her A Levels. She already had a provisional place at Cambridge, but when she heard we were going to get married she threw all that up and went off to share a flat with another girl.' Mrs Dearborn's fingers had returned to the compulsive fraying of the cords while her cigarette burnt itself out on the rim of the ashtray. 'She has an allowance under her father's will, a thousand a year. I don't know if she ever worked.'

'You never hear from her?'

'Oh, yes, we made up our quarrel in a sort of way. We were never like we used to be. She was always reserved and she became terribly secretive. I suppose that was my fault. I don't want to go in for a display of self-pity, Mr Wexford, but I had rather a lot to bear in my first marriage and then widowhood wasn't easy. I rather taught Isa to keep—well, a stiff upper lip, and not show her feelings.'

Wexford nodded. 'But she kept in touch with you by phone or by letter?'

'She'd phone me from time to time but she would never come here and she refused to tell me where she was living after she had left the flat she shared with the other girl. She phoned from call boxes. It made me very unhappy and Stephen saw it and then—then he got some private detective to find out where she was. Oh, it was so terrible! Isa swore she'd never speak to me again. She said I'd ruined her life. After that I tried not to let Stephen know I was worried about her and that's why I asked you to come here while—while he was out.'

'When did you last hear from her?'

She crushed out the smouldering cigarette stub and lit another. 'I'd better tell you a bit more about it all. After Stephen ran her to earth like that she phoned me to tell me I'd ruined her life, I didn't hear a word for months. Then, about a year ago, she started phoning quite regularly again, but she wouldn't say where she was living and she always sounded unhappy.'

'You must have commented on that?'

'Of course I did. She'd always said, "Oh, it's nothing. The world's not a very jolly place, is it? You taught me that and it's true." Mr Wexford, you don't know her. You don't know how impossible it is to question her. She just says, "Let's leave that, shall we?" I wanted her to come and see me at Christmas to tell her about . . .'

He raised his eyebrows a fraction. 'Excuse me, if I don't tell you what that something was. It can't have anything to do with Isa being missing. Anyway, I begged her to come and she did come. She came on Boxing Day. That was the first time I'd seen my daughter for nearly three years. And after that she came again, two or three times, but always when Stephen was out.'

'She saw him on Boxing Day'?

Melanie Dearborn shook her head. 'No, he spent the day with his mother. She's in a nursing home. Isa looked very thin and pale. It frightened me. She was never vivacious, if you know what I mean, but all the life seemed to have gone out of her. But she began to phone me regularly, about once a week. The last time I heard from her—that was what you wanted to know, wasn't it?—the last time was Friday a week ago. Friday, February 25th.'

Wexford felt the blood go from his face. He hoped it didn't show. 'She phoned you last Friday week?'

'Yes, at lunchtime. She knows Stephen's never in for lunch and she always phoned at about one-fifteen.'

11

Other rocks there be lying hid under the water, which therefore be dangerous.

WEXFORD sat quite still. He knew that her observant eyes would detect any unease that he might show. He could hear a clock ticking in the room, a sound he had not previously noticed Mrs Dearborn's fingers made a rending noise as they tore another half-inch of piping out of the chair. Picking feverishly, she went on talking.

'Isa sounded tremendously happy. There was a note in her voice I hadn't heard there since she was a little girl. She actually asked me how I was and how Alexandra was. Then she said she thought she'd soon have some news that would please me. Of course I asked her what news and she said she thought that could wait for a week or two, but she'd phone me again in a few days. Well, I couldn't bear to leave things like that, and I was begging her to tell me when the pips went on the phone. I said to give me her number and I'd call her back, but before she could they'd cut us off.'

It all fitted. It fitted horribly. 'She didn't phone you again?' he said, knowing what the answer would be.

'No, it was a terrible let-down. I went almost mad with—well, curiosity, I suppose you'd call it and I forgot all about not chasing her and I tried to phone Stephen to get him to find her again if he could. . . . But he was out all that afternoon and when he did come home I'd cooled off and I thought I'd just wait until she phoned again. But she hasn't phoned since.'

'What are you afraid of?'

'Of her happiness.' She laughed a little shrilly. 'Doesn't that sound absurd? I keep asking myself if happiness hasn't made her do something reckless, take some awful risk.' With a shiver, she said. 'What shall I do? Tell me what to do.'

Come to Kenbourne Vale with me and identify a body. He couldn't say that. If this had been Kingsmarkham and he in charge of the Morgan case, he would have said something like that but in the gentlest possible, the most roundabout way. He wasn't in Kingsmarkham and before he did anything he would have to talk to Howard, perhaps find out more before he did even that.

Melanie Dearborn had suffered a lot in her forty years. If his present assumption was correct, all the pain she had ever been through would be nothing compared with the anguish she was going to have to bear. He wouldn't wish it on his worst enemy. And this woman wasn't that. He liked her; he liked her femininity and her concern and her good manners.

What harm would it do to comfort her and let things slide for a bit? He had no duty here. He was on holiday.

'It's only just over a week, Mrs Dearborn,' he said. 'Remember there was a time when you didn't hear from Isa for months.'

'That's true.'

'If I may, I'll call on you again on Wednesday and if you still haven't heard by then, we'll report your daughter as a missing person.'

'You really think I'm making a mountain out of a molehill?'

'I do,' he lied. So what? He could be wrong, couldn't he? Isa—what was her other name?—could be alive and well and junketing about Europe with some boy for all he knew. Something like this had happened to him once before. He had *known* the girl was dead, all the evidence had pointed to it, and then she had turned up, all tanned and smiling from a holiday in Italy with a poet.'

'What's your daughter's surname?' he asked.

'Sampson,' said Mrs Dearborn. 'Louise Sampson, or Isa or Lulu or whatever she's calling herself at present.'

Or Loveday? Don't, he wanted to cry—he who had always rejoiced at positive identifications—don't make the thing worse for me, more definite.

'I must go.'

'How?' she asked. 'Taxi? Bus?'

'One of those,' he smiled.

'Let me drive you. You've been so kind, giving up your holiday time to me, and I've got to go shopping.'

They argued. Mrs Dearborn won. She went upstairs to fetch the baby and when she reappeared at the head of the stairs, Wexford went up to help her with the carry cot. Her head resting on a pale pink pillow, the child Alexandra stared up at him with large, calm blue eyes. She was rather a fat baby, exquisitely clean and dressed in an expensive-looking, one-piece garment of pink angora.

Mrs Dearborn tucked a white fur rug round her. 'My husband's latest extravagance,' she said. 'He buys presents for this child practically every day. She's got far more clothes than I have.'

'Hallo,' said Wexford to the baby. 'Hallo, Alexandra.' She behaved after the manner of her kind by first wrinkling her face threateningly, then allowing it to dissolve into a delightful smile of friendliness and trust. 'She's beautiful,' he said sincerely.

Mrs Dearborn made no reply to this. She was groping under coats on the hallstand. 'I'm looking for a scarf,' she said half to him, half to herself, 'a blue silk one I'm rather fond of. Heaven knows where it's got to. Come to think of it, I haven't seen it for weeks. I wonder if Stephen could have given it to the cleaning woman I had before this one? When she left he insisted on giving her masses of clothes. He's such an impulsive man.' The baby began to whimper. 'Oh, Alexandra, don't *start*. She's like a dog,' said Mrs Dearborn rather crossly, 'Once she knows she's going out she won't let you rest till you're up and away. I may as well borrow Stephen's coat. My fur's at the cleaners and it's so cold, isn't it?'

She enveloped herself in Dearborn's sheepskin jacket which was much too big for her and they ran to the car through a sudden downpour. Child and cot were dumped on the back seat as if they were luggage to be safely stowed and then forgotten. Wexford was rather surprised. He had judged Mrs Dearborn as a strongly maternal woman, wrapped up in her husband and her daughters. She wasn't too old to have a baby, but perhaps she was too old to enjoy caring for one. And yet she was no older than the sergeant's wife who even enjoyed playing with her baby when he woke her in the night. It must be her worry over Louise which all-consuming, withdrew her from the rest of her family.

'Tell me the name of the friend Isa shared a flat with,' he said.

'Verity Bate. They were at school together and Verity went to train as a teacher at St Mark and St John.'

'I take it that that's in London?'

'We're not half a mile from it now,' said Mrs Dearborn. 'It's quite near where you're staying, in King's Road. I'll show you. She'll be in her last year now, but I don't know if she's still in the flat. It's near Holland Park and I did try ringing the number, but I didn't get any reply.'

By now they had crossed the King's Road and were going nothwards. On the back seat Alexandra was making soft gurgling sounds. Wexford looked over his shoulder and saw that she was watching the rain slapping against the window, reaching out a fat hand as if she thought she could catch the bright glittering drops. They came into the Fulham Road by way of Sydney Street, and when they had passed the cinema and entered that part of the road which is as narrow as a country lane, Mrs Dearborn asked him if he would mind a few minutes delay.

'I always buy my bread and cakes here,' she said. 'Could you bear if if I left you with Alexandra?'

Wexford said he could bear it very happily. She parked the car by a meter in Gilston Road, exclaiming with satisfaction because its last occupant had left ten minutes still to run, and walked off to the cake shop without a parting word to the baby. Wexford turned to talk to her. She didn't seem at all put out at being left alone with a stranger, but put up her hands to explore his face. The rain drummed on the car roof and Alexandra laughed, kicking off the white rug.

Playing with the baby passed the time so pleasantly that Wexford almost forgot Mrs Dearborn and he was surprised when he saw that ten minutes had gone by. Alexandra had temporarily lost interest in him and was chewing her rug. He looked out of the window and saw Mrs Dearborn, deep in conversation with another woman under whose umbrella they were both sheltering. She caught his eye, mouthed, 'Just coming,' and then the two women approached the car.

Mrs Dearborn seemed to be pointing out the baby to her friend, if friend she was. From what he could see of her through the streaming rain as she pressed her face against the rear window, Wexford thought her an unlikely sort of acquaintance for a company chairman's wife. Her umbrella was a man's, of cheap uncompromising black, her shabby coat black, and underneath it she wore what looked like an overall. An old felt hat, jammed hard down on her head, partly hid her face but couldn't conceal the disfiguring mole between cheek and left nostril. He fancied he had seen her somewhere before.

Just as he was wondering how long they could bear standing there and gossiping in a downpour which had become a tempest, the woman in black moved off and Mrs Dearborn jumped into the car, slicking back her wet hair with her wet hands.

'I'm so sorry to have kept you. You must be wishing you'd taken that taxi. But you know how it is when you run into people and there's a very . . .' She stopped quite suddenly. 'Now, let's get you home,' she said.

'You were going to show me St Mark and St John.'

'Oh, yes. Can you see that sort of round building right down there to the left? Just before you get to Stamford Bridge? That's St Mark's library. The college grounds go right through to the King's Road. Are you going to talk to Verity?'

'I expect so,' Wexford said. 'At any rate, she can tell me where Isa went after she left her.'

'I can do that,' Melanie Dearborn said quickly. 'Don't forget that's where Stephen found her. It's in Earls Court. I'll write down the phone number. I'd phone it myself, I'd try to talk to Verity, only . . .' She hesitated and added rather sadly, 'None of her friends would tell *me* anything.'

Outside the house in Theresa Street they stopped and Mrs Dearborn wrote the number down for him. For half an hour her thoughts had been distracted from her daughter, but now he noticed that the hand which held the pen was shaking. She looked up at him, nervous again, her brow furrowed with anxiety.

'Are you really going to try and trace her for me? I'm a bit —I remember what happened when Stephen . . .'

'I'll be discreet,' Wexford promised, and then he said good-bye, adding that he would see her without fail on Wednesday.

The house was empty. Denise had left him a note, propped against a crystal vase of freesias, to say that they had gone out to buy a blackberry poncho. He wasn't sure whether this was something to wear or something to eat.

He phoned the Holland Park number, but no one answered. Now for girl number two, the witness perhaps to Dearborn's clumsy and tactless trapping.

A young man's voice said hallo.

'Who occupied the flat before you?' Wexford asked when he had explained who he was.

'Don't know. I've been here four years.'

'Four years? Louise Sampson was living there a couple of years ago.'

'That's right. With me. Lulu and I lived here together for— Oh, four or five months.'

'I see.' This little piece of information was doubtless one which Dearborn had thought it wise to keep from his wife. 'Can I come and see you, Mr . . . ?'

'Adams. You can come if you like. Not today, though. Say tomorrow, about seven?'

Wexford put the phone down and looked at his watch. Just gone five. The rain had dwindled to drizzle. What time did these college classes end for the day? With any luck, Verity Bate might just be leaving now or, better still, living in hall for her final year.

He found the big gates of the college its students call Marjohn's without difficulty. There were a few boys and girls about on the forecourt, embryo teachers, who gave him the kind of glances his generation— but not he—reserved for them, the looks which ask, Why are you wearing those curious clothes, that hairstyle, that outlandish air? He was convinced that no one in the King's Road wore his kind of clothes or was as old as he. He went rather tentatively into the porter's lodge and asked where he could find Miss Verity Bate.

'You've just missed her. She came in to see if there were any letters for her and then she went off home. Are you her dad?'

Wexford felt rather flattered. Suppose he had been asked if he were the girl's grandfather? 'I'll leave a note for her,' he said.

Before he went any further he really ought to tell Howard. His nephew had a force at his command, a force who could trace Louise Sampson in a matter of hours, match her with Loveday Morgan, or else show the two girls to be—two girls. But how much more satisfying it would be if he on his own could present Howard with a *fait accompli*, the checking and tracing all done. . . .

12

*The truth shall sooner come to light . . . whiles he
helpeth and beareth out simple wits against the false
and malicious circumventions of crafty children.*

'A NOTHER one of your women on the phone,' said Denise
rather nastily.

Wexford was just finishing his breakfast. He felt relieved that
Howard, who had gone to the study to fetch his briefcase, and
Dora, who was making beds, hadn't heard the remark. He
went to the phone and a girl's voice, breathless with curiosity,
said this was Verity Bate.

It was only eight-fifteen. 'You didn't waste any time, Miss
Bate.'

'I had to go back to Marjohn's last evening to fetch
something and I saw your message.' The girl went on smugly,
'I realised it must be very important and, as I've got a social
conscience, I felt I should get in touch with you as soon as
possible.'

Couldn't wait to know what it's all about, more like,
thought Wexford. 'I'm trying to trace someone you used to
know.'

'Really? Who? I mean, who can you possibly . . . ?'

'When and where can we meet, Miss Bate?'

'Well, I've got this class till eleven-thirty. I *wish* you'd tell
me who it is.' She didn't express any doubts as to his
identity, his authority. He might have been a criminal lunatic

102

bent on decoying her away. 'You could come to my flat . . . No, I've got a better idea. I'll meet you at a quarter to twelve in Violet's Voice, that's a coffee place opposite Marjohn's.'

Howard made no comment, asked no questions, when he said he wouldn't be in until after his lunch with Sergeant and Mrs Clements. Perhaps he was glad to be relieved of his uncle's company for the morning or perhaps he guessed that Wexford was pursuing a private line of enquiry, in current parlance, doing his own thing.

He got to Violet's Voice ten minutes before time. It was a small dark café, almost empty. The ceiling, floor and furniture were all of the same deep purple, the walls painted in drug-vision swirls of violet and lavender and silver and black. Wexford sat down and ordered tea which was brought in a glass with lemon and mint floating about in it. From the window he could see St Mark's gates, and before he had begun to drink his tea he saw a diminutive girl with long red hair come out of these gates and cross the road. She was early too.

She came unhesitatingly up to his table and said loudly, 'It's about Lou Sampson, isn't it? I've thought and thought and it must be Lou.'

He got to his feet. 'Miss Bate? Sit down and let me get you something to drink. What makes you so sure it's Louise?'

'She *would* disappear. I mean, if there's anyone I know who'd be likely to get in trouble or have the police looking for her, it's Lou.' Verity Bate sat down and stuck her elbows on the table. 'Thanks, I'll have a coffee.' She had an aggressive, rather theatrical manner, her voice pitched so that everyone in the café could hear her. 'I haven't the faintest idea where Lou is, and I wouldn't tell you if I had. I suppose it's Mrs Sampson tracking her down again. Mrs Dearborn, I should say. One thing about that woman, she never gives up.'

'You don't like Mrs Dearborn?'

The girl was very young, very strict and very intolerant. 'I don't like deceit. If my mother did to me what she did to Lou I'd never speak to her again.'

'I'd like to hear about that,' said Wexford.

'I'm going to tell you. It's no secret, anyway.' Verity Bate was silent for a moment and then she said very seriously, 'You do understand, don't you, that even if I knew where Lou was, I wouldn't tell you? I don't know, but if I did I wouldn't tell you!'

Equally seriously, Wexford said, 'I appreciate that, Miss Bate. Your principles do you credit. Let me get this quite straight. You don't know where Louise is, you've no idea, and you won't tell me because it's against your principles.'

She looked at him uncertainly. 'That's right. I wouldn't help Mrs Samp—Dearborn or *him*.'

'Mr Dearborn?'

Her white skin took a flush easily and now it burned fiery red, earnest and indignant. 'He was my dad's best friend. They were in partnership. Nobody ought ever to *speak to him again*. Don't you think the world would be a lot better place if we just refused to speak to people who behave badly? Then they'd learn bloody awful behaviour doesn't pay because society won't tolerate it. Don't you agree with me?'

She was more like fifteen than twenty-one. 'We all behave badly, Miss Bate.'

'Oh, you're just like my father! You're resigned. It's because you old people compromise that we're in the mess we're —well, in. Now I say that we ought to stop sending people to prison for stealing things and start sending people to prison who destroy other people's lives. Like Stephen Bloody Dearborn.'

Wexford sighed. What a little talker she was! 'He seems quite a pleasant man to me,' he said. 'I gather Louise didn't like him much, though.'

'*Like him*?' Verity Bate pushed back her hair and thrust her face forward until little sharp nose and large blue eyes were perhaps six inches from him. 'Like him? You don't know anything, do you? Lou worshipped that man. She was just so crazy about Stephen Dearborn it wasn't true!'

This statement had the effect on him she had evidently hoped for. He was profoundly surprised, and yet, when he considered it, he wondered why he hadn't arrived at the truth himself. That it was the truth, he had no doubt. No normal clever girl leaves school at a crucial stage in her school career, throws up a university place and cuts herself off almost entirely from her mother just because her mother has made a proper and entirely suitable marriage with a man to whom the girl herself has introduced her.

'She was in love with him?' he asked.

'Of course she was!' Verity Bate shook her head until her face was entirely canopied in red hair, but whether this was in continuing wonder at her own revelation or at Wexford's obtuseness, he couldn't tell. The hair flew back, driven by a sharp toss. 'I'd better tell you the whole story and mine will be an unbiassed account, at any rate. It's no use you talking to Stephen Dearborn, he's such a liar. He'd only say he never thought of Lou in that way because that's what he said to my dad. Ooh, he's *disgusting*!'

'This—er, unbiassed account of yours, Miss Bate?'

'Yes, well, we were at school together, Lou and I, in Wimbledon. That's where my parents live, and Lou and Mrs Sampson lived in the next street. Stephen Dearborn was living up in ghastly Kenbourne Vale and Dad used to bring him home sometimes on account of him being what dad called a poor lonely widower.'

'He was married before, then?'

'His wife died and their baby died. That was all centuries ago. Stephen was supposed to be fond of kids and he used to take me out. Tower of London, Changing of the Guard, that sort of crap. Oh, and he dragged me around Kenbourne Vale too, showing me a lot of boring old architecture. It's a wonder I didn't catch something awful in that slum. When I got friendly with Lou, he took us both.'

'How old were you?'

'Sixteen, seventeen. I had to call him Uncle Steve. It makes me feel sick when I think of it, physically sick.' Her mouth turned down at the corners. 'Lou's not like me, you know. She keeps everything below surface, but it's all there, emotion welling and churning like a . . .' The childish voice dropped thrillingly. '. . . a cauldron! Anyway, we all went out together but I was the odd one. Stephen and Lou—well, it was like in the days when people had chaperones. I was their chaperone. And then one night when she was staying at my place she told me she was in love with him and did I think he loved her? It gave me quite a shock, Lou telling me anything about her personal life. I didn't know what to say, I didn't understand it. I mean, she was seventeen—maybe eighteen by then—and he was middle-aged. You can't imagine a girl of eighteen falling for a man of forty, can you?'

'It happens.'

'I think it's urky,' said Miss Bate with what looked like a genuine shudder. 'The next thing was she asked him back to her place. To meet,' she added darkly, 'her mother.'

Wexford had almost forgotten that the purpose of this talk had been to discover Louise Sampson's whereabouts. He was seeing the little cameo again, the stranger entering the house alone—because an unmannerly girl had left him to introduce himself—then, searching for the girl's mother, had come upon a half-open door and seen in a kitchen a woman in a white apron engaged in an age-old feminine task. The girl's strident voice jerked him out of his daydream.

'Lou and I were due to sit for our A's, but the week before they started Lou didn't come to school. I phoned her place and her mother said she wasn't well. Then one night my dad came in and said to Mummy, "What d'you think, Steve's going to marry the Sampson girl." Of course, I thought he meant Lou, but he didn't. Fancy calling a woman of thirty-seven a girl! Lou never took her A's. She was really ill, she had a sort of nervous breakdown '

'A case of *filia pulchra, mater pulchrior,*' said Wexford.

'I wouldn't know. I never did Latin. They sent Lou down to her grandmother and then they got married. I left school and started at Marjohn's and Daddy said he'd pay half the rent of a flat for me if I could find another girl to share and I was sort of looking for someone when Lou rang up from this grandmother's and said she'd never go to those two in Chelsea, and could she share with me?'

'How long did that last?'

'About a year. Lou was more shut in than ever. She was heartbroken. Her bloody mother used to phone and pretend to me it was all rubbish about Lou fancying Stephen. Anyway, Lou got fed up being hunted and she went off to share with someone in Battersea. I'm not telling you the address, mind you.'

'I wouldn't dream of asking you, Miss Bate.'

'After that we sort of lost touch.'

'You couldn't bear to see so much suffering, was that it?'

'Exactly.' She seemed relieved at so pat a solution which perhaps avoided for her the necessity of explaining that she hadn't bothered to phone and never wrote letters. 'Louise Sampson,' she said dramatically, 'went out of my life. Perhaps she's found happiness, perhaps not. I shall never know.' She lifted her chin and stared intensely in the direction of the coffee machine, showing to Wexford a delicate and faintly quivering profile. He wondered if she had attended all or some of the films shown at the Garbo season, a recent offering, according to Denise, of the Classic Cinema up the road. 'That's all I can tell you,' she said, 'but if I knew any more I wouldn't reveal a single word.'

Surely the sergeant's wife didn't go to all this trouble, a full dinner service, linen napkins, side plates and all, when her husband popped home alone for a bite to eat? Wexford was sure she didn't but he behaved as if all this ceremony was normal and even forgot his diet.

He was aware that further pomp was to attach to the entry of the child, delayed until after their coffee, not only for the sake of suspense but to prove Mrs Clements' ability to be a gracious hostess though a mother. It was touching, he thought, the way she kept stoically to the theme of their conversation—

inevitably, with her husband taking part, the general decadence of modern life—while listening surreptitiously for a squeak from the next room. At last, when Clements and Wexford had left the table and were standing at the picture window, contemplating Kenbourne Vale from twelve floors up, she re-entered the room with the baby in her arms.

'He's got two teeth,' she said, 'and not a bit of trouble cutting them.'

'A fine boy,' said Wexford. He took the child from her and talked to him as he had talked to Alexandra Dearborn, but James responded less happily and his shining dark eyes grew uneasy. An adopted child, Wexford thought, might well show signs of insecurity, handled as he must have been since leaving his true mother by stranger after stranger. 'He's a credit to you,' he said, and then to his shame he found his voice thick with an unlooked-for emotion. It was out of his power to say more.

But he had said enough, or his expression had told what he couldn't say. Mrs Clements beamed. 'I've waited fifteen years for this.'

Wexford handed the boy back. 'And now you've got fifteen years of hard labour.'

'Years and years of happiness, Mr Wexford.' The smile died. Her full, rather dull, face seemed on an instant to grow thinner. 'If—if they'll let me keep him.'

'She's signed an affidavit, hasn't she?' said the sergeant fiercely. 'She's promised to give him up.'

His wife gave him a wifely look, part compassion, part gentle reproof. 'You know you're as worried about it as I am, dear. He was more worried than me at first, Mr Wexford. He wanted to—well, find out who she was and give her some money. To sort of buy James, you see.'

'I don't know much about adoption,' said Wexford, 'but surely it's illegal for money to pass in the course of these transactions?'

'Of course it is,' said Clements huffily. He looked put out. 'I wasn't serious.' His next words rather belied this remark.

'I've always been a saver, I daresay I could have raised quite a bit one way and another, but I . . . You don't think I meant it, sir?'

Wexford smiled. 'It would be a bit too risky, wouldn't it?'

'Breaking the law, you mean, sir? You'd keep the child but you'd always have the fear of being found out hanging over you.'

Clements was never very quick on the uptake, Wexford thought. He said, 'But would you have the child?

'Of course you would, sir. You'd have brought it from the natural mother, in a manner of speaking, thought it doesn't sound very nice put that way. You'd offer her a thousand pounds, say, not to oppose the making of the order.'

'And suppose she took the money and agreed and opposed the order just the same? What redress would you have? None at all. You couldn't ask her to sign an agreement or enter into a contract as any such transaction in matters of adoption would be illegal.'

'I never thought of that. An unscrupulous sort of girl might even engineer it so that she could get hold of money to support her child.'

'She might indeed,' said Wexford.

13

But in Utopia every man is a cunning lawyer . . .

SHE too had had a baby . . . During the past year Loveday
Morgan had had a baby. If Loveday Morgan was Louise
Sampson, Louise had had that baby. A good reason, added to
the other good reasons, for not letting her mother see her until
Christmas when she might have been fully recovered from the
child's birth.

Now that birth must have been registered, but not, apparently,
to a mother called Morgan. Surely Louise wouldn't have
dared register the child in a false name? The penalties for
making false registrations were stated clearly enough, Wexford
knew, in every registrar's office. They were more than suf-
ficient to daunt a young girl. She would have registered it in
her own name.

This, then, was what he just had to check on before he went
any further. This might mean he need go no further. But his
plan was doomed to postponement, for he was no sooner in
his own office when Howard phoned through to request his
presence at a house in Copland Road.

'Mrs Kirby?' Wexford said. 'Who's she?'

'Gregson was mending her television at lunchtime on February 25th. She's just phoned to say she's remembered something we ought to know.'

'You won't want me.'

But Howard did. He was very pressing. When Wexford

joined him at the car and noted the sullen presence of Inspector Baker, he saw it all. Tactful pressure had been brought to bear on Baker to include the chief inspector in this visit. A king-size sledge-hammer, indeed, to swat a fly, unless the fly itself had suddenly developed into a far larger insect. Evidently Baker didn't like it and not on these grounds alone. He gave Wexford a cold penetrating stare.

And Wexford himself was annoyed. He would have been far happier making his own private researches. Howard had arranged it to avoid hurting his uncle and Wexford was there to avoid hurting his nephew, but all they had succeeded in doing was to upset Baker thoroughly. The nape of his neck, prickly with ginger bristles, had crimsoned with anger.

Wexford wondered about his private life, the solitary existence he must lead somewhere, perhaps in a trim suburb in a neat semi-detached which he had furnished for the young wife who had deserted him. He could hardly imagine a greater humiliation for a middle-aged man than that which Baker had suffered. It would dig into the very roots of his manhood and shake what should, at his age, have been a well-adjusted personality.

He was sitting beside the driver, Wexford in the back with his nephew, and since they had left the station no one had uttered a word. Now Howard, trying to ease the tension, asked Baker when he would be moving from Wimbledon into the new flat he was buying in north-west London.

'Next month, I hope, sir,' Baker said shortly. He didn't turn his head and again the dark flush had appeared on his neck.

The mention of Wimbledon reminded Wexford of Verity Bate who had said that her parents and, at one time, the Sampsons had lived in that suburb. So it was there that the inspector's trouble had come upon him. Not discouraged, Howard pressed the point, but Wexford had the impression that Baker only replied because Howard was his superior officer. And when the superintendent spoke next of the week, terminating on February 27th, that Baker had taken off to

111

consult with solicitor's and arrange with decorators, Baker's shrug was almost rude.

'I'm afraid you're one of those people who never take a proper holiday, Michael,' Howard said pleasantly. 'Even when you were supposed to be off you were hanging about Kenbourne Vale nearly every day. Is it such an attractive place?'

'Filthy hole,' Baker said abruptly. 'How anyone could live here beats me.'

From the tensing of the driver's shoulders, Wexford guessed that he was one of those who did. Here was another instance of the inspector putting people's backs up, literally this time. A gloomy silence fell. Howard deliberately avoided catching his uncle's eye and Wexford, embarrassed, looked out of the window.

It was a damp, raw day, and although it was still early afternoon, lights showed here and there behind long sash windows, making pale bright rectangles in the grey façades. The air itself seemed grey, not dense enough for fog but laden with a damp which blackened the pavements. Kenbourne Vale wore the colours of a snail shell, glimmering faintly in a snail's pallid, dull hues, under the ashen sky which seemed to have dropped and to lie low and sombrely over it. Church spires, a stadium, sprawling factories loomed before the car, took solid shape and then dissolved again as they passed. Only the new office blocks, strident columns of light, had a positive reality in the thickening gloom.

They entered Copeland Hill, that district which, nearly a week before, had been Wexford's gateway to his nephew's manor. Much had happened since then. He asked himself how he would have felt on that bus last week if he had known that today he would be riding in a police car with Howard, honorary yet treated by Howard with honour, to interrogate an important witness. The thought cheered him and, viewing Copeland Road with quickening interest, he resolved not to let Baker deter him or damp his ardour.

This was one of the streets which Dearborn had his eye on, and Wexford saw that a whole section of the left-hand terrace was undergoing renovation. Scaffolding covered it and men were painting the broad lofty expanse a rich cream colour so that the moulding above the windows was revealed as swags, bunches of grapes and lovers' knots. New railings of curled wrought iron rested against the scaffolding, ready to be fixed to the balconies.

The effect of this half-completed conversion was to make the neighbouring houses look even shabbier than they would otherwise have done. But neither the scars of decay nor the unmistakable signs that each was inhabited by a score of ill-assorted tenants rather than one prosperous family could quite ruin their stateliness. Garmisch Terrace was mean now and had been mean in the spirit of its conception; this place had a strange indestructible beauty because, like an old woman who had once been a pretty girl, its bones were good.

Mrs Kirby who occupied part of the ground floor of a house whose plaster front was scored all over with long river-like cracks, had also once been pretty in the Yorkshire of her girlhood. Her accent marked her as a native of the East Riding, and Wexford wondered what combination of circumstances had brought her to Kenbourne Vale. She was about sixty now. Apparently she owned a lease of the whole house, but lived in only three rooms of it which she kept as neat and sparkling as a pin.

He marvelled at her ordinariness. This place seemed curious to him, the broad street, the mansions like ornamented and windowed cliffs fascinating and wonderful, and he thought they must seem so to her too with her background. What did she think of the people in their exotic clothes, the black faces, the defiant boys and girls who lived in the warren above her head? She conducted her life as if she still lived in some Yorkshire cottage, it seemed, from the description she gave them in minute detail of the way she had spent February 25th. An early riser, she had got up at seven, cleaned the flat, chatted over the fence to a neighbour. Loquaciously, she took the three policemen round the shops with her, listed the dishes prepared for her lunch and came finally, while Baker tapped an impatient foot, to the arrival of Gregson sharp at twelve-thirty.

'Aye, it were half past twelve when he come. I know that on account of that's when I have my bit of dinner and I thought to myself, some folks have no consideration. I said to him, How long will you be? and he said half-an-hour so I put my plate in t'oven, not liking to have folks watch me eating.'

'When did the phone call come?' Howard asked.

'Must have been after one.' She pronounced the last word to rhyme with 'on'. 'Aye, because I recall thinking, you're taking a long half hour, lad. I heard t'phone ring and I answered it and this girl says, Can I speak to Mr Gregson. It's t'shop.'

'You're sure that's what was said, "the shop"?'

'Nay, I can't be sure. Might have been Sytansound or whatever they call theirselves. I called t'young lad and he talked to her, just said yes and no and good-bye. Then he finished t'job and off he went.'

'Be more precise about the time of the call, Mrs Kirby.'

She enjoyed being precise. Wexford could see, and see Howard also saw, that to her precision and accuracy were not the same thing. Her eyes flickered doubtfully. She wanted to impress, to earn praise, even if she did so through a precise inaccuracy.'

Baker said, 'If you thought it had been a long half hour Mrs Kirby, it must have been a while after one. Five or ten minutes.'

Wexford longed for the power to say like a judge to counsel, 'Don't lead, Mr Baker.'

The leading had done its work. 'Aye, about ten past,' said Mrs Kirby, and hopefully, 'Near a quarter past.'

Baker smiled in silent triumph. Smile on, thought Wexford. Loveday didn't phone Gregson, she phoned her mother. He spoke at last. Howard's encouraging glance permitted him a question. 'Did you recognise the girl's voice?'

'Nay, why would I?'

'Well, presumably you phoned the shop yourself to tell them your set wanted attention.'

'Aye, I did, and I phoned them last back end too, but I never talked to any girls. It was always that manager, that Gold.'

'Let him lie his way out of this one,' said Baker as they trooped into Sytansound where, on a dozen lambent screens, goblin puppets cavorted for the entertainment of the under-fives. Behind the desk which had been Loveday's was a fifty-year-old lady in boots and knee-breeches who swam out to them, followed by fat lumbering Gold.

'There wasn't any girl in the shop after ten to one on that Friday,' said Gold, unhappy at these frequent visits from the law.

'Where is he?' said Baker.

'Out the back with the van.'

A high brick wall made the van park gloomy. Behind it, Wexford knew, was the cemetery. He could see the trees over the top of it. You couldn't get away from that cemetery in Kenbourne Vale; it was the heart and soul of the place.

Gregson had heard them coming. He was leaning against the wall, his arms folded, waiting for them. The pose was defiant, but his face was frightened.

'He doesn't talk, you know,' Howard said conversationally to his uncle as Baker approached the boy. 'I mean, he literally doesn't open his mouth. He told Baker he didn't go out with the girl and where he was on Friday night, and since then he just won't talk.'

'The best defence. I wonder who taught him that?'

'I wish I knew. I only hope his mentor isn't giving lessons to all the villains in Kenbourne.'

Gregson had let his arms fall to his sides because Baker told him to and moved a few inches from the wall. He answered the inspector's questions only with shrugs. In his thin denim jacket he looked cold and pinched and very young.

'We're going to have a talk, my lad,' said Baker. 'Down at the station.'

Gregson shrugged.

At the police station they took him into an interview room. Wexford went upstairs and contemplated his gasworks. The gasometer had deflated quite a lot to reveal behind it a canning factory, a church and a building that was probably Kenbourne town hall. He thought about girls who were fond of romantic names, about babies who didn't look like their parents and then about Peggy Pope and her lover. He came to no conclusions.

His phone rang. Howard's voice said, 'Gregson's scared stiff of us. How about you having a go at him?'

'Why should he talk to me?'

'I don't know, but it can't do any harm.'

It didn't do any good either. Gregson chain-smoked. He made no answers to any of Wexford's questions. Wexford asked him if he knew what sort of a man Harry Slade was, that his word couldn't be relied on (not quite true, this), if he was aware of the implication of the phone call he had received at Mrs Kirby's. Gregson said nothing. It was, in its way, an admirable performance. Real hardened criminals, twice Gregson's age, couldn't have kept it up.

Wexford tried bullying, although it went against the grain with him. He stood over the boy and bawled questions into his ear. Gregson smelt of the sweat of fear but still he didn't speak. His cigarettes were all gone and he held his hands clenched on the table in front of him.

The stuff of martyrs, Wexford thought. In Sir Thomas's day they would have put him to the rack and the thumbscrew. He cooled his voice and went back once more to the telephone call. Who was the girl? He knew there was no girl in the shop at that time, didn't he? At that precise time Loveday Morgan had made a call. The call was to him, wasn't it?

Wexford leant across the table. He fixed his eyes on Gregson, forcing the boy to look at him, and then, shockingly, Gregson spoke. It was the first time Wexford had heard his voice, a thin cockney whine. 'I want a solicitor,' he said.

Wexford went outside, called in D.C. Dinehart, and told Howard what had happened.

116

'That's bloody marvellous,' said Baker. 'That's all we need.'

'If he wants a solicitor he'll have to have one,' said Howard. 'Someone's been showing him the ropes all right.'

'Mr. Wexford perhaps.' Baker could hardly conceal his rage. 'Telling him his rights, no doubt.'

Taking a leaf out of Gregson's book, Wexford said nothing. They went back into the interview room and Howard asked the boy which solicitor he wanted.

'I haven't got one,' said Gregson. 'You can bring me the phone book.'

14

If any man had rather bestow this time upon his own
occupation, he is not letted or prohibited.

IT was half past six before Wexford got away. Howard was
still closeted with a certain Mr de Traynor who smoothly
and sympathetically referred to Gregson as 'my youthful
client here.' Gregson had picked him out of the phone book
because he liked the sound of his name.

There was more than a name to Mr de Traynor. His silky
eyebrows almost disappeared into his silky hair when he heard
that as yet no charges had been made against Gregson, that,
in fact, no one was quite ready to charge him, and he settled
down to teach Howard about the law.

'Am I to understand that my youthful client here has
actually been detained for no less than three hours . . . ?'

Avoiding Baker, Wexford slipped out by a back way he
had discovered which led him into a paved alley. On one side
of it was a building that looked like a section house, on the
other rows of newly-built garages used for housing police cars
and vans. It was all on a much grander scale than anything in
Kingsmarkham, and a few days before it would have had an
oppressive, even deterrent, effect on him. But now neither the
size of the place nor Baker's unjust attitude troubled him much.
Human nature was the same here as in the country, and it was
by studying human nature and patterns of behaviour rather
than relying solely on circumstantial evidence that he had had

his successes in the past. He told himself as he walked briskly in the direction of Kenbourne Lane that he had the edge on Baker, for he had never and would never compose a solution to a mystery and then manipulate facts and human nature to fit it. Pity, though, that he had missed his chance of going to Somerset House.

Rather than rely on finding a bus that would take him to Earls Court, Wexford made for a tube station he had seen from the police car. It wasn't called Kenbourne Vale but Elm Green. Something to do with those famous, long-felled trees about which Dearborn had discoursed? There were no elms now, only a wide grey pavement full of people scurrying towards the station under fluorescent lights, and inside a maze of long tiled passages.

When he came to change at Notting Hill Gate he got into the wrong train. Half an hour had passed before he finally alighted at Earls Court and by then he was fighting claustrophobia, the blood pounding in his head. How did Londoners stick it?

Nevern Gardens turned out to be another of those huge squares, tall houses glaring at each other across rows of parking meters and plane trees with branches like waving threads. He found Lewis Adams on the third floor of one of these houses, in an absurdly narrow, absurdly long, room with a tiny kitchen opening out of it, and he wondered why it was this curious shape until he realised it was a walled-off segment of a huge room, perhaps now divided into five or six shoe boxes like this one.

Adams was eating his evening meal, a Chinese concoction of beansprouts and bamboo shoots and little red bones heaped on a soup plate and balanced on his knees. On the table in front of him was a glass of water, a bottle of soy sauce and a plate of pancakes which resembled chunks of pink foam rubber.

But if his eating arrangements were Bohemian, the room he had shared with Louise Sampson was not. A well-vacuumed red carpet covered the floor, cared-for paperbacks filled the bookshelves, a large television set faced the twin armchairs and the window overlooked the tops of plane trees.

'You'd better ask me questions,' said Adams. 'I don't know what it is you want.' He spoke economically. His voice was cultured and controlled with the tone of a budding barrister or a medical student preparing to sit for triumphant finals. But he looked too young for that, as young as Gregson and not unlike him. Smallish and neat, he had fair-brown hair which stopped short at the lobes of his ears. He would tell exactly what he wanted to tell, no more and no less, Wexford thought. There would be no reiteration here of grandiloquent principles, no juvenile drama.

'Where did you meet her?' he asked.

'She came into the restaurant where I was a waiter.' Adams didn't give a deprecating smile or apologise for his past (perhaps present) humble calling. He finished his beansprouts and set the plate to one side. 'We talked. She said she was sharing with a girl in Battersea, but she wasn't comfortable because they only had one room and the girl had her boy friend there at nights. I asked if she'd like to share with me.' Still without smiling, he added, 'I was finding the rent a bit much.'

'She agreed?'

'The same day. She collected her stuff and moved in that night.'

Wexford was rather shocked. Did they really go on like that these days? 'A bit cold-blooded, wasn't it?'

'Cold-blooded?' Adams hadn't understood and when he did he was more shocked than Wexford had been. His face went cold with disgust. 'You're not suggesting she slept with me, are you? *Are you*?' He shook his head, tapping one finger against his brow. 'I don't understand your generation. You accuse us of being promiscuous and casual and so on, but you're the ones with the unclean minds. I honestly don't care if you believe this or not, but Lulu lived here with me for four months and we were never lovers. Never. I suppose you're going to ask why not. The answer is that these days, whatever happened in your time, you can sleep in the same room

120

as a girl and not want to make love to her because you're not frustrated. No one any longer has the power to force you into an unnatural celibacy, you're free to have the girls you do want. We didn't attract each other, that's all, and we weren't in the position of having to make do with any port in a storm.' He held up one hand. 'I'm not queer. I had girl friends. I went to their places. No doubt Lulu saw her boy friends at theirs.'

'I believe you, Mr Adams.'

At last he smiled. Wexford saw that delivering his little lecture had relaxed him and he wasn't surprised when he said, 'Don't call me that. My name's Lewis. People used to call us Lew and Lulu.'

'Did Lulu work?'

'She had some money of her own, but she worked sometimes. She used to go out cleaning. Why not? You *are* conventional. It's well paid around here and what you get you keep. No cards, no stamps, no tax.'

'What was she like, what sort of a girl?'

'I was fond of her,' said Adams. 'She was quiet and sensible and reserved. I like that. You get sick of the sound and the fury, you know. Her stepfather,' he added, 'was a great guy for sound and fury.'

'He came here?'

'She'd been here four months.' Adams took a drink from the glass of water on his dinner tray. 'She opened the door and when she let him in I heard her give a sort of cry—I was out in the kitchen through there—and say, "Stephen, darling Stephen, I knew you'd come for me one day".' He shook his head disapprovingly both, Wexford thought, at the hysterical utterance itself and at hearing it on his own lips. 'It wasn't like her, losing control. I was shattered.'

'But he'd only come to find out where she was?'

'He explained that. You know all those endless explanations people go in for. I didn't care for him, a big showy man, an extrovert. Lulu didn't say much. She told me afterwards that when she saw him she really believed he wanted her at last

121

and the shock of knowing he didn't for the second time was too much for her. He thought what you thought, that I was her lover. He made a fuss about that. I didn't deny anything or defend myself. Why should I? Then there was a very nasty scene which is best forgotten and he went.'

'What was the scene about?'

Adams had now adopted a manner rather at odds with his youthful appearance. It was as if the young barrister had become an elderly and successful counsel who, conducting an unsavoury case, reveals because he must for his client's sake the bare facts, while taking pains to omit and make it clear that he is omitting all the nauseating details.

'How can knowing that possibly help you?'

'Anything about Louise might help. I can't make you tell me, but I think you should.'

Adams shrugged. 'I suppose you know your own business best. This stepfather—I don't know his name, I'm afraid, Stephen Something—was telling Lulu in a very tactless way how happy he and her mother were when Lulu said, "You're very fond of children, aren't you, Stephen?" And he said he was and he hoped to have some of his own. Lulu suddenly became rather like a powerhouse. I don't want to dramatise things, but she gave the impression of very strong pressure holding down an irrepressible force.'

Powerhouses, Wexford thought, cauldrons . . . A frightening sort of girl, intimidating as are all those passionate and turbulent creatures with no outlet for their fevers. 'She said something to him?'

'Oh, yes. I said it was nasty. She said, "Not with my mother you won't, Stephen. Surely she didn't forget to tell you she had a hysterectomy when I was fifteen?"' Adams' face creased with distaste. 'I left them then and went out into the kitchen. The stepfather screamed and shouted at her and Lulu did some screaming too. She didn't tell me what they said and a week later she left.'

'Where did she go?'

'She wouldn't tell me. We weren't on very good terms when

we parted. Pity, because we'd always trusted each other. Lulu didn't trust me any more. I'd told her off for shouting at this Stephen. She thought I was sympathising with her parents and that I'd tell them where she was if she told me.'

'You must have some idea,' Wexford protested.

'From various things she said, I think she went to Notting Hill. Possibly to a boy friend.'

'His name?'

'There was someone who used to phone her. Somebody called John. He used to ask for her and say, This is John.'

In the morning he asked to see everything Loveday Morgan had worn on the day of her death, and they showed him bra and tights from a chain store, black shoes, black plastic handbag, lemon acrilan sweater and sage green trouser suit. He saw too the contents of that handbag and every personal article found in her room.

'No cheque book?'

'She wouldn't have had one, sir,' said Sergeant Clements, putting on the indulgent look he kept for this naive old copper who thought every female corpse had been of the landed gentry. 'She hadn't any money, bar her wages.'

'I wonder what's become of the child's birth certificate?'

'With Grandma,' said Clements firmly. 'Grandma's blind or in the laughing house or she'd have come forward by now. Any thing else you want to see, sir?'

'The scarf she was killed with.'

Clements brought it in on a kind of tray.

'She's supposed to have been wearing this?' Wexford queried. 'It's a very expensive scarf. Not for a girl earning twelve pounds a week.'

'They have their funny extravagances, sir. She'd go without her dinners three or four days and then blue a pound on a scarf.'

Slowly Wexford handled the square of silk, exposing the label. 'This is a Gucci scarf, Sergeant. It didn't cost a pound. It cost eight or nine times that.'

Clements' mouth fell open. Who connected with this case, Wexford thought, but Mrs Dearborn would have an expensive silk scarf? Hadn't she been hunting for this very scarf before she went out on Monday afternoon? She hadn't been able to find it because her daughter had borrowed it, without saying anything in the way daughters do, on her last visit to Laysbrook House.

15

The sage gravity and reverence of the elders should keep the youngers from wanton licence of words and behaviour.

HOWARD was taking part in a top-level conference at Scotland Yard, discussing no doubt what the next move should be now that Gregson had made his escape under the protection of the ingenious Mr de Traynor. No matter how omnipotent Howard might appear to be, Wexford knew he was in fact answerable always to the head of his Divisional Crime Squad, a commander who very likely knew nothing of a country chief inspector's arrival on the scene.

The gasworks loured at him through a veil of drizzle. He paced up and down, fretting, waiting for Pamela to phone through and say when Howard would be back. He had to talk to Howard before going to Laysbrook House, and he half hoped he wouldn't have to go at all. His wishes in the matter of Louise Sampson were curiously divided. He liked Mrs Dearborn and the humane man in him wanted to see her come out of the mortuary weeping with relief instead of white with shock. But he was a policeman too, whose pride in his abilities had recently suffered blows. Considerable experience and hard work had gone into matching the missing girl with the dead. He knew his desire was base, but he admitted to himself that he would feel a thrill of pride if he vindicated himself in Baker's view and saw Howard's eyes narrow with

admiration. And she had, after all, to be someone's daughter
. . .

He jumped the way Melanie Dearborn jumped when the
phone rang, but instead of Pamela's, the voice was a man's
and one couldn't remember having heard before.

'It's Philip Chell.'

Wexford took a few seconds to remember who this was. 'Oh,
yes, Mr Chell?'

'Ivan said to tell you he's got something for you.'

That bloody *Utopia*, Wexford thought. But it wasn't.

'It's something he's found out. He says, d'you want him to
come to you or will you come here?'

'What's it about?' Wexford asked impatiently.

'Don't know. He wouldn't say.' The voice became ag-
grieved. 'He never tells me anything.'

'Will tomorrow morning do? About ten at your place?'

'Make it eleven,' said Chell. 'If he knows we've got a
visitor he'll have me up at the crack of dawn.'

Pamela put her head round the door. 'Mr Fortune will be
free at twelve, sir.'

An hour to wait. Why shouldn't he go to Garmisch Terrace
during that hour instead of waiting until tomorrow? Whatever
Teal had to tell him might provide another link between
Loveday and Louise. He took his hand from the mouthpiece
and said, 'How about if I were to . . . ?' but Chell had rang
off.

The front door was open and he walked straight in. For once
the hall was crowded. Chell, in fetching denim and knee-
boots, was leaning against the banisters reading a picture
postcard and giggling with pleasure. Peggy sat on one corner of
the large hall table among newspapers and milk bottles, holding forth shrilly to the Indian and the party-giving girl, while
Lamont, the baby in his arms, stood disconsolately by.

Wexford gave them a general good morning and went up to
Chell, who, when he saw who it was, switched off his preoccupied smile like someone snapping off a light.

126

'Ivan's gone out for the day,' he said. He gave the post-card a last fond look and slipped it into his pocket. 'I can't tell you anything. All I know is Ivan was going through his cuttings when he suddenly said, "My God," and he must get hold of you.'

'What cuttings?'

'He's a designer, isn't he? I thought you knew. Well, people write about him in the papers and when they do he cuts the bit out and pastes it in his book.'

Aware that Peggy had fallen silent and that by now every-one was listening avidly, Wexford said in a lower tone, 'Could we go up and have a look at this book?'

'No, we could *not*. Really, whatever next? Ivan would *kill* me. He was perfectly horrid to me before he went out just because I'd left last night's washing up. I can't help it if I have these frighful migraines, can I?'

The party girl giggled.

'I feel very depressed,' said Chell. 'I'm going to draw out my whole month's allowance and buy some clothes to cheer myself up.' He stuck up his chin and marched out, banging the front door resoundingly behind him.

'All right for some,' said Peggy, passing a dirty hand across her face and leaving black streaks on her beautiful brow. 'Nice to be a kept man, isn't it, Johnny?'

'I look after her, don't I?' Lamont muttered, giving the baby a squeeze to indicate to whom he was referring. 'I've done everything for her practically since she was born.'

'Except when you're down the pub.'

'Three bloody hours at lunchtime! And you go out leaving me stuck with her every evening. I'm going back to bed.' He hoisted the baby on to his shoulder and made for the base-ment stairs, giving Peggy a backward glance which, it seemed to Wexford, contained more of hurt love than resentment.

'Look, Mr What's-your-name,' said Peggy, 'when are you lot going to open up Loveday's room so as we can re-let it? The landlords have lost fourteen quid already and it's keeping them awake at nights.'

'Is there someone wanting to rent it?'

'Yeah, her.' Peggy pointed to the party girl who nodded. 'Funny, isn't it? Big laugh. A guy like you would pay seven quid a week *not* to live in it.'

'It's two pounds a week less than what I'm paying,' said the other girl.

'Well, I'm not discussing the landlords' business in public,' said Peggy huffily. She jumped down from the table and tucked a milk bottle under each arm. 'You'd better come with me down to the hole in the ground.'

Wexford followed her, murmuring vainly that the matter wasn't in his hands. In the basement room Lamont was lying on the bed, staring at the ceiling. Peggy took no notice of him. She began to rummage among letters on the mantelpiece.

'I'm looking for a bit of paper,' she said, 'so you can write down who they have to contact about getting the room back.'

'Will this do?' 'This' was a sheet of paper he had picked up from the top of an untidy pile on the foot of the bed. As he held it out to her he saw that it was an estate agent's specification of a house in Brixton, offered for sale at four thousand, nine hundred and ninety-nine pounds.

'No, it won't do!' said Lamont, rousing himself and seizing the paper which he screwed up and hurled into a sooty cavern behind the electric fire.

Peggy laughed unpleasantly at him. 'You said you were going to chuck that out—God, it must be the weekend before last. Why don't you clear up the place instead of slopping about on the bed all day? It's time you got up, anyway, if that guy's going to phone you about that TV work. Did you give him the number of the Grand Duke?'

Lamont nodded. He slid off the bed, sidled up to Peggy and put his arm round her.

'Oh, you're hopeless,' she said, but she didn't push him away. 'Here,' she said to Wexford, 'you can write the number down on the back of this envelope.'

Wexford wrote down the number of the police station and of

128

Howard's extension and, glancing at his watch, saw that the hour was up.

The superintendent had spread before him photographs of the carefully restored and made-up face of Loveday Morgan, taken after death. The eyes were blue, the hair light blonde, the mouth and cheeks pink. But to anyone who has seen the dead, this was the modern version of a death mask, a soulless painted shell.

' "Life and these lips have long been separated",' Wexford quoted 'You wouldn't show these to her *mother*?'

'We haven't found a mother to show them to.'

'I have,' said Wexford and he explained.

Howard listened, nodding in slightly hesitant agreement. 'She'd better be brought here,' he said. 'We'll need her to identify the body. It'll be best if you go for her and take Clements and maybe a W.P.C. with you. I think you should go now, Reg.'

'I?' Wexford stared at him. 'You don't expect me to go there and . . . ?'

He felt like Hassan who can just bear the idea of the lovers being tortured to death out of his sight, but revolts in horror when Haroun Al Raschid tells him they must be tortured in his house with him as an onlooker.

Howard was no oriental sadist. He looked distressed, his thin face rather wan. 'Of course, I can't give you orders. You're just my uncle, but . . .'

'But me no buts,' said Wexford, 'and uncle me no uncles. I'll go.'

He phoned her first. He had promised to phone her. A thin hope, a thin dread, made him ask, 'You haven't heard from Louise?' He looked at his watch. Just after one, the time she would hear if she was going to.

'Not a word,' she said.

Break it gently, prepare the ground. 'I think I may . . .' Made cowardly by her anxious gasp, he said, 'There are some people I'd like you to talk to. May I come over straight away?'

'Baker said we'd never identify her,' said Howard. 'This'll shake him. Don't look so miserable, Reg. She has to be someone's child.'

Clements drove. They went through Hyde Park where the daffodils were coming out.

'Bit early, isn't it?' Wexford asked out of a dry throat.

'They do things to the bulbs, sir. Treat 'em so that they bloom before their natural time.' Clements always knew everything, Wexford thought crossly, and made all the facts he imparted sound unpleasant. 'I don't know why they can't leave things alone instead of all this going against nature. The next thing they'll be treating cuckoos and importing them in December.'

In the King's Road all the traffic lights turned red as the car approached them. It made the going slow and by the time Clements turned in under the arch to Laysbrook Place, Wexford felt as sick as he had done thirty years before on the day he took his inspector's exams. The brickwork of Laysbrook House was a pale amber in the sun, it's trees still silver-grey and untouched by the greening mist of spring. But the forsythia was a dazzling gold and the little silvery clusters he had noticed among the snowdrops now showed themselves as bushes of daphne, rose pink bouquets dotted all over the lawn. It was all very quiet, very still. The house basked in the thin diffident sunlight and the air had a fresh scent, free from the fumes of diesel to which Wexford had grown accustomed.

A young, rather smart, cleaning woman let him in and said, 'She told me you were coming. You're to go in and make yourself at home. She's upstairs with the baby, but she'll be down in a tick.' Was this the new char who stole things, who might have—but had not—made off with a Gucci scarf? The police car caught her eye and she gaped. 'What about them?'

'They'll stay there,' said Wexford, and he went into the room where Dearborn had shown him the maps and his wife had opened her heart.

16

*I know how difficult and hardly I myself would have
believed another man telling the same, if I had not
presently seen it with mine own eyes.*

HE didn't sit down but paced about the room, hoping that
she wouldn't keep him waiting for long. And then, suddenly in the midst of his anxiety for her, it occured to him
that once the girl was positively identified, the case would
be solved. Things didn't simply look black for Stephen
Dearborn. Louise Sampson had been murdered and who
could her murderer be but Dearborn, her stepfather?

The motive now. He had better get that clear in his mind.
And there was plenty of motive. Since he had talked to Verity
Bate he had never doubted the sincerity of Louise's love for
Dearborn, but he had supposed that Dearborn had been
speaking the truth when he told Mr Bate that he hadn't
returned it. Perhaps, on the other hand, he *had* originally
been in love with Louise or had at least some strong sensual
feeling towards her, a feeling which had lost some of its force
when he met the mother. Of course, it was the reverse of the
usual pattern, this preference of a man for an older woman
over a young girl, but Wexford didn't find it hard to imagine.
Anyway, a man could love two women at once. Suppose
Dearborn had married the mother because she was more completely to his taste, while retaining the daughter as a mistress
he couldn't bring himself to relinquish? Or their affair could

have started after Dearborn found her at Adams' flat, by which time he might have been growing weary of his wife.

In that case Dearborn was almost certainly the father of her child. Wexford sat down heavily when it occurred to him that the child could be Alexandra. Until now he hadn't thought much about Louise's announcement, reported by Adams, that her mother couldn't have children. After all, Louise had said she was only fifteen at the time. She could have got it wrong and have taken some minor surgery for the far more serious and final operation. If she had been speaking the truth, Melanie Dearborn couldn't be Alexandra's mother. But Dearborn could have brought home his own child—his and Louise's—to be adopted by himself and Louise's mother. And Melanie wouldn't have to know whose it was, only that it was a child whom Dearborn had adopted through a 'third party'. You didn't have to adopt through a society.

Alexandra, an adopted child . . . Or rather, adopted by one of her parents. That would account for the mother's indifference and the father's—the real father—passionate obsession.

But where was she all this time? Why didn't she come down? He heard her footsteps moving briskly overhead but he heard no other sound. Louise could have threatened Dearborn, especially if he had begun to cool off her, with exposure to her mother of their affair and then of the identity of the child. A very real threat, Wexford thought. Louise hadn't just been young and his mistress, but his stepdaughter as well. Melanie would surely have left him if she had found out. A strong motive for murder.

That was a clever explanation he had come up with for his office number having been found in Louise's handbag. How much more likely, though, that she had it there because she phoned him at work habitually! Perhaps it was he whom she had phoned on February 25th . . . But no, it couldn't be, for on that day, at that time she had phoned her mother.

There was, of course, a good deal more to be worked out. Probably Mrs Dearborn could help him if only she would come down. He felt a return of anguish for her, deepened now by his strong suspicion of her husband's guilt. The footsteps stopped and Alexandra began to cry, but the sounds were those of a baby who is peevish rather than distressed. He looked at his watch and saw that he had been there for nearly a quarter of an hour. Perhaps he should find the cleaning woman and ask her to ...

The door swung open and Mrs Dearborn walked in. She was more smartly dressed than on the previous occasions when he had seen her, her hair was brushed and lacquered and her face carefully made up. The baby was in her arms.

'Oh, Mr Wexford, I'm terribly sorry to have kept you waiting.' She freed one hand and held it out to him. 'My poor little girl is having such trouble with her teeth. I was trying to get changed and comfort her at the same time. I see you've brought reinforcements,' she said, and joked, 'Don't worry, I'd have come quietly.'

Have come? Did she mean she couldn't come? He wished she didn't look so happy and carefree, cradling the baby and stroking her head with a tenderness he had thought she lacked. 'Mrs. Dearborn,' he began, 'I want you to ...'

'Sit down, Mr Wexford. You can sit down for a moment, can't you?'

Uneasily he lowered himself on to the edge of one of the mutilated chairs. It is hard enough to break bad news to anyone at any time, but to break it to someone as cheerful and pleased with life as Melanie Dearborn looked now ... ? 'We really shouldn't delay,' he said. 'The car's waiting and ...'

'But we don't have to go anywhere. It's *all right*. My daughter phoned me. She phoned me as soon as you rang off.'

His stomach seemed to turn over, the way it sometimes did when he was in a lift, and a faint sweat broke out in the palms of his hands. He couldn't speak. He could only stare stupidly at her. She smiled at him triumphantly, her head a little on one side. Some of her joy at last communicated itself to

133

Alexandra, who stopped crying, rolled over on to her back on the sofa cushion and gave a crow of laughter.

'Are you sure?' he said, and his voice was a croak. 'Sure it was your daughter?'

'Of course I'm sure! You'll see her if you wait a while. She's coming this afternoon. Isn't it marvellous? Isn't it?'

'Marvellous,' he said.

'The phone rang and I thought it was you, calling back for something or other.' She spoke quickly, chattily, quite unaware of the shock she had given him. 'I picked it up and I heard the pips. As soon as I heard them I *knew*. Then she said, "Hallo, Mummy." Oh, it was wonderful! I tried to get in touch with you but you'd already left. I just sat down and ate an enormous lunch—I haven't been able to eat properly for days—and then I went upstairs and got all dressed up. I don't know why.'

Wexford gave her a stiff, sickly smile. Alexandra laughed at him, kicking her legs in the air.

'Will you stay and see her?'

'No. I don't think anyone would doubt your word on this, Mrs Dearborn. I'll go and tell the sergeant not to wait, and then if you'd just give me a few details . . .'

Clements was treating the policewoman to one of his lectures, waving his hands as he pontificated on change and decay, Utopias and Dystopias, past glory and contemporary decadence. Wexford put his head through the car window.

'Tell Mr Fortune it's no dice. The girl's turned up.'

'Oh, great!' said the policewoman sincerely.

Clements wagged his head up and down with a kind of grim gratification. He started the car. 'She'll have a tale to tell, you can bet on that, and bring home a load of trouble for mother to sort out.'

'Give it a rest, can't you?' Wexford said savagely, knowing he shouldn't speak like that to a man who had been kind to him and hospitable and who liked him, but he hadn't been able to help himself. He saw Clements' face go red and truculent with hurt and then he went back into the house.

Alexandra was chewing voraciously at her teething ring while her mother fetched smoked salmon and a bottle of asti spumante out of her husband's fancy dining refrigerator, setting it all on a tray. Killing the fatted calf, he thought. Thou art ever my daughter and all that I have is thine . . .

'Where had she been? What was all that disappearing act about?'

'She's going to get married. It's this boy, John. I suppose she's been living with him.' Mrs Dearborn sighed. 'They've had their ups and downs, but it sounds as if they really love each other. He's married but separated from his wife—awful, isn't it, to be married and separated before you're twenty-five? He's getting a divorce under the new act. Isa knew that last time she phoned but she wouldn't tell me until he'd got his decree in case something went wrong. That's Isa all over always cautious, always secretive. She sounds so happy now.'

He smiled stiffly. She probably thought he disapproved. Let her. The realisation that he had been hopelessly wrong, the shock of it, was only just beginning to hit him where it hurt. An awful desire to run away had seized him, to run to Victoria and get on a train and go home. He couldn't remember ever having made such a monumental howler before and the memory of how he had talked so eagerly to Howard, had nearly convinced him, made him go hot all over.

And now, as he looked back, he saw that although certain circumstances in the lives of the two girls had seemed alike or coincidental, Loveday had never really matched Louise. He asked himself whether a wealthy girl brought up like Louise would have shown horror when asked to a party or baulked at being taken into a pub; if such a girl would have scuttled off for comfort to a non-denominational church; if Louise, who had been Dearborn's friend before he was her mother's, would have needed to carry his office number in her handbag, a number she must long have known by heart. He knew it was all impossible. Why hadn't he known before? Because he had so desperately wanted to prove his abilities, and in order to do so had sacrificed probability to wild speculation. He had been

135

guilty of the very sin he had laid at Baker's door, that of formulating a theory and forcing the facts to fit it. Fame had been more important to him than truth.

'Good-bye, Mrs Dearborn,' he said, and he added hollowly, 'I'm very glad for you.'

She shook hands with him on the doorstep but she didn't look at him. She was looking past him towards the arch. And she hadn't long to wait. As Wexford crossed Laysbrook Square, he saw the girl coming from the King's Road direction, saw her disappear under the shadows of the arch, a slim fair girl but otherwise quite unlike Howard's photograph of the dead.

Angrily cursing himself for an idiot, he walked for miles about Chelsea. Soon he would have to face Howard. By now Clements would have told him and he would be reflecting how unwise he had been to let family feeling and sentimentality persuade him into seeking his uncle's help. Baker would be told and Baker would shake his head, inwardly derisive.

At last he went home to Theresa Street, hoping there would be no one there, but both women were at home and a third with them, Denise's sister-in-law, who asked after his health, told him he could expect nothing else at his age, and assured him she could get any number of copies of *Utopia* he might desire from her bookshop.

'We all make mistakes, Reg,' said Howard gently when they sat down to dinner. 'And, Reg . . . ? We're not all competing for some sort of national forensics certificate, you know. It's just a job.'

'How many times have I said that, or something very like it, to my own men?' Wexford sighed and managed a grin. 'You can laugh if you like, but last week I really had some sort of idea that I was going to step in and solve the baffling case that eluded the lot of you. An elderly Lord Peter Wimsey. You were going to sit back and gasp in admiration while I expounded.'

'I daresay real life and real police work aren't like that.'
He might have added, Wexford thought, that his uncle had,
however, given them some useful tips. But he hadn't really,
so Howard couldn't. Instead he said almost as generously,
'I'd have felt the same if I'd come down to your manor.'

'It's odd, though, how convinced I was about that girl.'

'And you convinced me, but Baker would never go along
with it. I know you don't like him and I admit he's a peculiar
character, but the fact is he seldom does make mistakes. Even
when his wife went off and there was that business about the
unborn child, he went emotionally to pieces but his work
didn't suffer. If he says Gregson's guilty—and he's got a bee
in his bonnet about it—the probability is Gregson *is* guilty.'

Wexford said rather sourly, 'He doesn't seem to be getting
very far with proving it.'

'He's a lot further than he was. He's breaking up that
Psyche club alibi. Two of the men who were there with Harry
Slade have cracked and admitted they never saw Gregson
after eight o'clock. And another thing. Slade's girl friend—
remember the one he was supposed to be playing Monopoly
with last Saturday?—she's got a record. Baker's having another go at Gregson now without, we hope, the damping presence of Mr de Traynor.'

Wexford took two of his tablets and noticed how far the
level in the bottle had gone down. No one could say he had
failed there, at any rate.

'I don't think I'll come in with you tomorrow, Howard,'
he said. 'We're off on Saturday and there'll be the packing
and . . .'

'Come off it. Dora will do all that.' Howard surveyed his
uncle's burly figure. 'Besides, the only thing you could pack
is a punch.'

Wexford thought of Lamont. Had he avoided seeking a
further interview with him because he was physically afraid?
Perhaps. Suddenly he realised how deeply his illness had de-
moralised him. Fear of getting tired, fear of getting wet, fear
of being hurt—all these fears had contributed to his failure.

Wasn't it really fear of over-exerting himself that had made him waste the morning at Garmisch Terrace rather than go to Somerset House where a quick examination of records would have prevented today's *faux pas*? Kenbourne Vale police station was no place for him and Howard, for all his kindness, knew it.

'Well, I seem to have time on my hands for once, Reg. May as well catch up on my reading and dip into those Russian short stories my sister-in-law brought round. Curious stuff, but interesting, don't you find? One of these days I'd like your opinion . . .'

Literary chit-chat.

Four short stories and two hours later, Howard got up to answer the phone. Gregson had confessed, Wexford thought. The relentless Baker, Baker with the bee in his bonnet, had finally broken him.

But when Howard came back into the room, he could see from his nephew's face that it wasn't going to be as simple as that.

Howard didn't look at all pleased. 'Gregson's bolted,' he said. 'Baker was having a go at him in that Psyche Club, Gregson apparently doing his customary dumb act, when suddenly he found his fists if not his tongue, clouted Baker one and made a getaway in a stolen car. Baker fell off the bar stool and cut his head open on, of all things, a glass of advocaat.'

'Oh, poor Mr Baker!' said Denise, coming in from the kitchen with a white urn full of African violets.

'You weren't supposed to be listening. Here, let me take that thing, or give it to Reg. It's too heavy for you.'

'Gregson shouldn't take you too long to find,' said Wexford.

'God, no. He'll be under lock and key by morning.'

'Will you have to go over to Kenbourne, darling?' asked Denise, still hugging the urn.

'Not me. I'm going to bed. My days of running round in

138

squad cars chasing little villains are over. Will you mind that thing?'

Each put out his arms to grasp the urn which looked as if it weighed half a hundredweight. It was partly the idea that Howard had already got hold of it, partly a sudden terror of the effect on him of supporting so heavy a weight, that made Wexford draw back at the last moment. The urn crashed on to the carpet with a ponderous juddering thud, sending earth and broken leaves and pink and mauve petals flying against the walls and the pale hitherto immaculate Wilton.

Denise screamed so loudly that Wexford didn't hear Howard's hollow groan. Muttering apologies—although all apologies were inadequate—falling to his knees among the mess, he tried to scoop earth up in his hands and only made matters worse.

'At least the vase thing isn't broken,' he said stupidly.

'Never mind the bloody vase,' said Howard. 'What about me?' He had collapsed into a chair and was nursing his right foot. 'That landed fair and square on my toes.'

Denise had burst into tears. She sat in the middle of the wreckage and cried.

'I'm terribly sorry,' said Wexford miserably. 'I'd like to ... I mean, is there anything I can ... ?'

'Just leave it,' said Denise, drying her eyes. 'I'll see to it. Leave it to me. You go to bed, Uncle Reg.'

Ever polite, although he was white with pain, Howard said, 'Forget it. You couldn't help it, Reg. You're not fit enough to cope with things like that yet. No wonder you dropped it. God, my foot! I hope nothing's broken.'

He got his shoe off and limped towards the door. Denise fetched a dustpan and brush and began rescuing those of her plants that were still intact while Dora, summoned from upstairs by the uproar, picked grains of soil from the wallpaper.

Watching them disconsolately, Wexford reflected on his nephew's last remarks and upon their double meaning.

17

*You must not forsake the ship in a tempest because
you cannot rule and keep down the winds.*

I N the morning Howard's foot was worse, but he refused to
see a doctor, saying that it was imperative he arrived on
time in Kenbourne Vale.

'But you won't be able to drive, darling.' Denise had
stayed up until the small hours cleaning the carpet and she
had an exhausted air. Transferring her gaze from a large in-
eradicable stain to her husband's swollen instep, she said,
'You can hardly put that foot to the ground.'

'Never mind. I'll phone for a driver.'

'Unless Uncle Reg would . . .'

They looked at Wexford, Howard doubtly, Denise as if she
considered that anyone fit enough to reject yoghurt in favour
of bacon and eggs was quite capable of driving a car through
the London rush hours. Wexford didn't want to go. He had
lost all interest in the Morgan case, and plain cowardice over-
came him when he thought of meeting Baker and Clements,
both of whom would know of his exploded theory. Why had
he ever been so stupid as to go and poke about in the Montfort vault in the first place? Let Howard send for a driver.

He was going to plead a pain in his eye—and for the first
time in days he could feel it aching and pricking again—when
Dora said unexpectedly, 'Of course Reg will take you, dear.
It's the least he can do after dropping that thing on your

140

foot. He can come straight back and have a rest, can't you, darling?'

'Give me the keys,' said Wexford resignedly. 'I hope you realise I've never driven in London traffic.'

But it wasn't as bad as he had feared, and concentrating on being one of the honking, thrusting herd, charging wild beasts which made Kingsmarkham motorists seem like sheep, made him forget his eye and, briefly, that stronger trepidation. They arrived to find Gregson safe in a cell, having been discovered taking refuge at his sister's house in Sunbury. Howard, sure of him now on the grounds of assault on a police officer and of taking and driving away a vehicle without its owner's consent—offences which even Mr de Traynor couldn't dispute—limped off to talk to him. Wexford decided to make his escape and get home before the threatening rain began and he made for that semi-secret exit into the mews. It had occurred to him happily by this time that if Howard's injury was insufficient to keep him from work, Baker's wouldn't be, so he was much disconcerted when, marching confidently down one of the bottle-green caverns, he came face to face with the inspector, his head swathed in bandages.

There was nothing for it but to stop and ask him how he was feeling.'

'I'll survive,' Baker said curtly.

The only polite answer one can make to this churlish response is a muttered, 'I hope so.' Wexford made it, added that he was glad things were no worse and moved on. Baker gave a dry cough.

'Oh, Mr Wexford . . . ? Still got a few days of your holiday left, haven't you?'

This sounded like the first move towards a truce. Wexford's spirits were so low that he was grateful for any show of cordiality. 'Yes, I'm in London till Saturday.'

'You want to try and take in Billingsgate, then. Plenty of red herrings there, and you'll find the wild geese at Smithfield.'

Like a goose himself, Baker cackled at his joke. His laughter with an accompanying patronising pat on the shoulder didn't rob the remark of insult. It simply made it impossible for Wexford to take offence. Immensely pleased with himself, the inspector went into the lift and clanged the doors behind him. Wexford went down the stairs. No point now in avoiding the front entrance.

Suddenly it seemed even more futile to avoid Clements. There, at least, the deference due to rank would forbid any witticisms of the nature Baker had indulged in. Wexford came down the last flight and caught sight of his own reflection in a window which the brick wall behind it had transformed into a huge and gloomy mirror. He saw a big elderly man, a wrinkled man in a wrinkled raincoat, whose face in which some had discerned wisdom and wit, now showed in every line the frustrated petulance of a spoiled child and, at the same time, the bitterness of age. He straightened his shoulders and stopped frowning. What was the matter with him to let a small reverse get him down? And how could he stoop to comfort himself with his rank? Not only must he not avoid Clements, but must seek him out to apologise for his behaviour of the previous day and—this was even more imperative—say good-bye. Had he really thought of quitting Kenbourne Vale for ever without taking a formal leave of the kind sergeant?

The big outer hall was deserted but for the two uniformed men who presided over a long counter and dealt with enquiries. One of them courteously offered to see if the sergeant was in the building, and Wexford sat down in an uncomfortable black leather armchair to wait for him. It was still only ten o'clock. Rain had begun to splash lightly against the arched windows which flanked the entrance. Perhaps the meteorological office had been right in its forecast of a deep depression settling over South-East England. If the weather had been more promising, he might have telephoned Stephen Dearborn and reminded him of the tour he had suggested. It would be doing the man a favour rather than asking for one,

142

and Wexford felt he owed Dearborn something. Not, in this case, an apology—for you cannot apologise to a man for suspecting him of murder—but a friendly gesture to make up for harbouring such absurd and unfounded suspicions. Wexford was well aware of the guilt one can feel for even thinking ill of a man, although those thoughts have never found verbal expression.

He wasn't sure whether it was this reminder of his folly that made him go hot and red in the face or Clements' sudden appearance at his elbow. He rose to his feet, forgetting self-pity and self-recrimination. In a couple of hours Clements would be eating his lunch with his wife and James, his last lunch with James as a probationary father. Or his last lunch with James?

'Sergeant, I want to apologise for the way I spoke to you.'

'That's all right, sir. I'd forgotten all about it.'

Of course he had. He had other things on his mind. Wexford said gently and earnestly, 'Tomorrow's the great day, isn't it?'

As soon as he had spoken he wished he hadn't brought the subject up. Until this moment he had never quite realised the tension under which Clements lived and worked, the strain which daily grew more agonising. It showed now in the mammoth effort he made to keep his face ordinary and civilised and receptive, even stretching his mouth into a rictus smile. Wexford saw that he couldn't speak, that anxiety, invading every corner of his mind and his thoughts, had at last dried up that tide of moralising and censorious criticism. He was empty now of everything but the animal need to hold on to its young.

They stared at each other, Wexford growing embarrassed, the sergeant, all garrulity gone, dumb with panic and the dread of tomorrow. At last he spoke in a thick dry voice.

'I'm taking the morning off. Maybe the whole day.' He paused, swallowed. 'Depends on . . . My wife . . . On what they . . .'

'We shan't meet again, then.' Wexford held out his hand and Clements took it, giving it a hard painful squeeze as if it

143

were a lifeline. 'Good-bye, Sergeant, and all the very best for tomorrow.'

'Good-bye,' said Clements. He dropped Wexford's hand and went out into the rain, not even bothering to turn up his coat collar. A passing car splashed him but he didn't seem to notice. Small incidents such as this, which would once have inspired a diatribe against modern manners, no longer had the power to prick the surface of his mind.

Wexford stood on the steps and watched him go. It was time for him to go too, to leave Kenbourne Vale and Loveday Morgan and forget them if he could. Strange how absorbed he had been in trying to discover who she was, tramping around Fulham, weaving fantasies. Now as he looked back on the past week, he realised that he was no nearer knowing who she was or who had killed her or why than he had been when Howard had found him in the vault. It seemed to him that he had had a few sensible ideas, firm conclusions, which even that howler of his couldn't shake, but they had grown vague now and he had almost forgotten what they were.

Water which had gathered on the blue glass panels of the lamp above his head trickled down and dripped on him. He moved slowly down the steps and as he did so water hit him from another angle. A wave of it splashed against his trouser legs and he glanced up, affronted. The taxi, cause of the offence, had drawn up a few yards from him and directly in front of the police station. Its rear door opened and a vision in a purple silk suit with a white orchid in its buttonhole descended on to the wet pavement.

'What a day for the Honourable Diana's wedding,' said Ivan Teal when he had paid the taxi driver. 'And she such a sunny-natured girl. Where are the flunkeys rushing to meet me with umbrellas?'

'This isn't the Dorchester,' said Wexford.

'Don't I know it! I have some experience of police stations, principally West End Central. Were you on your way to see me?'

144

'See *you*?' In Wexford's present state of mind, Garmisch Terrace and the case seemed a world away. 'Was I supposed to be seeing you?'

'Of course you were. I told Philip to say ten. He knew I had this wedding at St George's. The bride's gown is one of mine so I must be in at the kill. When you didn't turn up I came to you. The wedding's at half eleven.'

'Oh, that,' said Wexford, recalling how Chell had side-tracked him with his talk of newspaper cuttings. 'It doesn't matter now. Don't you waste your time.'

Teal stared at him. His hair was carefully waved and gusts of Aphrodisia came from it and his suit. 'You mean you've found out who she was?' he said.

Wexford almost asked who. Then he remembered that to some people Loveday Morgan's death was important and he said, 'If you've got some information you'd better see Superintendent Fortune or Inspector Baker.'

'I want to see you.'

'It was never my case. I'm here on holiday and I'm going home on Saturday. You're getting rather wet, you know.'

'This tussore isn't exactly drip-dry,' said Teal, moving under the arch from which the blue lamp hung. 'I wish I'd gone straight to Hanover Square,' he grumbled. 'It's always hell getting a taxi in Kenbourne. Can you see if that one down there has got his light up?'

Wexford didn't bother to look. 'You said you wanted to see the superintendent.'

'You said that. I'm not over-fond of policemen. Remember? You're different. If I can't talk to you I'll be on my way.' Teal flung out a purple silk arm. 'Taxi!' he shouted.

The cab was going the wrong way. It waited for some lights to go green and, in defiance of regulations, began to make a U-turn. Behind it, looming scarlet through the downpour, appeared the bus that went to Chelsea.

'It was nice meeting you,' said Teal, going down the steps. 'Never thought I'd say that to a . . .'

The taxi drew up, the bus went by. 'You'd better come in a

minute,' said Wexford with a sigh. 'I can spare half an hour.'

Teal was never amiable for more than a few minutes.

'I can't spare that long myself,' he said with a return to asperity. 'Really, you're very inconsistent. What a ghastly place! No wonder policemen have a grudge against humanity. What's this? Some sort of annexe to the morgue?'

'An interview room.' Wexford watched him dust the seat of a chair before sitting on it. He supposed he ought to feel flattered. However highly one values one's profession, it is always a compliment to be told that one is better, more human, more sympathetic, less conventional, than the common run. But boredom with the whole business made him almost impervious to flattery.

'Comfy?' he said sarcastically.

'Oh, don't come that!' snapped Teal. 'Not you. You're not one of these flatfeet who think that because one's gay, one's got the mentality of a finicky schoolgirl. I'm going to a wedding and I don't want to muck up my clothes any more than you would.'

Wexford looked at him with positive dislike. 'Well, Mr Teal, what is it you want to tell me?'

'That minister we were talking about—remember? His name is Morgan.'

18

The priests whom they find exceeding vicious livers,
them they excommunicate from having any interest
in divine matters.

IT was like giving up smoking, thought Wexford, who had
given it up with some difficulty years before. The bloody
things made you ill, you resisted them, they even bored you,
but only let someone produce one—or, worse, light it under
your nose—and you were hooked again, yearning, longing to
get back to the old habit. Teal had done that to him, although
he hadn't lighted it yet. Wexford tried to suppress the excitement he felt, the hateful irritating excitement, and said:

'What minister?'

Maddeningly, Teal began to digress. 'Of course it's hind-
sight,' he said, 'but there was something funny about her
voice. I noticed it at the time and yet I didn't, if you know
what I mean. She didn't have any accent.'

'I don't have any accent,' said Wexford rashly.

Teal laughed at that. 'You mean you think you don't. You
can't hear that faint Sussex burr any more than I can hear
the rag-trade camp in my voice unless I listen for it. Just think
about it for a moment. Johnny talks R.A.D.A., Peggy South
London, Phil suppressed cockney with a gay veneer, your
superintendent pure Trinity. One doesn't have to be a Henry
Higgins to sort all that out. Everyone has an accent that he's
got from his parents or his school or his university or the
society he moves in. Loveday didn't have any at all.'

'What's that go to do with some minister?'

'I'm coming to that. I've thought about it a lot. I've asked myself who are these rare creatures that speak unaccented English. One example would be servants of the old school. I should think that when there was a whole servant class they all talked like that—flat, plain English without any inflexion or intonation. Their parents brought them up to it, having been servants themselves and knowing that cockney wouldn't be acceptable in a housemaid. Who else? Children brought up in institutions, maybe. People who spent years of their lives in hospitals and perhaps people who have spent all their lives in closed communities.'

Wexford was growing very impatient. 'Brought up in an institution . . . ?'

'Oh, come *on*. You're the detective. Don't you remember my telling you how she went to the temple of the Children of the Revelation?'

'She can't have been one of them. She worked in a television shop. They don't have television or read newspapers.'

'There you have it, the reason why her parents haven't got in touch. Didn't it occur to you? Anyway, her father couldn't have got in touch. He's that Morgan who was their minister and got put inside. He's in prison.'

There was a dramatic pause. Wexford had thought he could never care about this case again, never experience for a second time the thrill and the dread of the hunter with his quarry in sight. Now he felt the tingle of adrenalin in his blood, a shiver travel up his spine.

'I keep this book of press cuttings,' Teal went on. 'That is, I collect newspapers that have bits about me in them, but often I don't cut the bits out for a year or so and the papers accumulate. Well, a couple of nights ago, having time to kill, I started on my cuttings and on the back of a photograph of one of my gowns there was a story about this Morgan appearing in a magistrates' court.'

'You have the cutting with you?'

148

'Do me a favour, I'm on my way to a very fashionable wedding. As Wilde says . . .' Here Teal wriggled affectedly—purposely to annoy, Wexford thought—and said in a camp falsetto, 'A well-made dress has no pockets.' He chuckled at the chief inspector's discomfiture. 'Anyway, I stuck it in my book, court proceedings side downwards, of course. You can do some work now.'

'When did these proceedings take place, Mr Teal?' Wexford asked, keeping his temper.

'Last March. He was charged with bigamy, indecent assault on *five* women—the courage the man must have had! —and having had carnal knowledge of a fourteen-year-old girl. I don't know what that means precisely, but I expect you do. He was committed for trial to the Surrey Assizes.' Teal looked at his watch. 'My God, I mustn't be late and find myself in a rear pew. I want to get a good look at the Honourable Diana in all my glory.'

'Mr Teal, you've been very helpful. I'm grateful. There's just one other thing. You said Loveday asked you if Johnny and Peggy were trustworthy. What did she want to entrust to them?'

'To him, you mean. Herself, I suppose, if she was in love with him.'

Wexford looked doubtful. 'A woman of fifty might feel that way, but I don't think a young girl would. I'm asking myself what precious thing she had to entrust to anyone.'

'Then you must go on asking yourself, Mr Wexford, because I do have to go now.'

'Yes, of course. Thanks for coming.'

The interview room became a drab little hole again after Teal had gone. Wexford went out into the corridor and began to mount the stairs. It struck him suddenly that he could climb stairs now without getting short of breath.

It was a piece of luck really getting that information from Teal, for passing it on immediately would vindicate him in the eyes of Howard and Baker. Not that he had done anything but listen and that reluctantly. Never mind. He would tell them simply what Teal had told him and leave them to follow it up. Unless . . . Unless he delayed passing it on for half an hour, and used that half-hour to do a little research of his own in the police station library.

If they had one. At the top of the stairs he encountered someone he thought was Sergeant Nolan and asked him. They had. Down one floor, sir, and third door on your right.

In the library he found Pamela and D.C. Dinehart, each occupied with a newspaper file, and wearing on their young faces the serious and absorbed expressions of students in the British Museum. Both looked up to nod and then took no further notice of him. It took him no more than ten minutes to find what he wanted, the proceedings against Morgan in the Assize court.

The *News of the World* had dealt with the case lubriciously, yet with its customary manner of righteous outrage; *The People* had seen in it occasion for a venomous article on corruption among ministers of religion; *The Observer*, its nose in the air had tucked it away under a story about a blackmailed county councillor. For facts and photographs he selected *The Sunday Times* and the *Sunday Express*.

Alexander William Morgan had been separated from his wife for some years before the commission of the offences, he lodging next door to his church in Artois Road, Camberwell, she remaining in the erstwhile matrimonial home in nearby Ivy Street. Apparently, the rift had taken place when Morgan received a call and became shepherd of the Camberwell Temple. He had tried, very gradually, to infuse into the bitter and life-denying creed of the Children of the Revelation a certain liberalism, although, due to the opposition of diehard elders, had got no further than to make a few of them believe that television and radio enjoyed in the privacy of their own homes was no sin.

In sexual matters he had been more successful. Indeed, his success had been startling. A stream of young women had given evidence, including a 'Miss Hannah Peters whom he had

150

married (gone through a form of marriage was the charge) in a ceremony of his own devising at which he had been both bridegroom and officiating priest. The other girls, even the fourteen-year-old, regarded themselves as his wives under the curious philosophy he had propounded to them. He had treated them affectionately. They said they had expected, as a result of what he had told them and by reason of his relationship with them, to inherit a more blissful form of eternal life than the less favoured Children. It was only when he made advances to older women that his propensities had come to light. Morgan had been sent to prison for three years, still protesting that he was responsible for conferring on these women a peculiar grace.

Wexford noted down the names of all the women witnesses. Then he studied the photographs, but only one of them caught his eye, a picture of the temple itself in Artois Road. He glanced up and, seeing that Pamela had finished her researches, beckoned her over.

'Are you going back to Mr Fortune's office?'

She nodded.

'He has a snapshot of Loveday Morgan . . .'

'Yes, sir, I know the one you mean.'

'I wonder if you mind asking him if he'd have it sent along to me here?'

That was that, then. It was the only way. Howard would, of course, come back with the snapshot himself, note from the newspaper stories that Morgan had two daughters, and the case would pass out of his, Wexford's, hands. He felt rather flat, for he had found her in such an undramatic way.

While her waited for Howard to appear, he looked at the other photographs, round-faced, bespectacled Morgan, forty six years old, a suburban satyr; Morgan with his wife and two fat little girls, either of whom might have been Loveday in childhood; Hannah Peters, plain, smiling, a bride among the handmaidens with an Alice band holding back her frizzy hair.

He smelt Pamela's floral perfume and looked round to find her at his elbow.

'Mr Fortune has gone to court, Mr Wexford, and he's left a message to say he's going straight on to St Biddulph's Hospital to get his foot X-rayed.'

'But you've brought the snapshot,' Wexford said slowly.

'It was on his desk, sir, and since you wanted it, I'm sure he wouldn't . . .'

'Thank you very much, Pamela,' said Wexford.

His hand was trembling oddly as he took it from her and placed it beside the *Sunday Express* photograph of Morgan's temple in Artois Road. Yes, it was as he had thought. The newspaper picture showed the whole church, the snapshot only a corner of it, but in both were the same dusty shrubs nudging a brickwall, the same ridge of coping, and what had seemed in the snapshot to be a wooden post was now revealed as a segment of a door.

There was no girl in the newspaper shot, Morgan, Wexford was sure, had posed the girl—his daughter? one of his 'brides'?—in front of the temple and taken the photograph himself. He returned the snapshot to Pamela and left the library, deep in thought.

What now? Follow Pamela and leave a message for Howard, his reasonable self told him. Or see Baker. The inspector would soon be back from the court. Wexford revolted from the idea of confiding in him and seeing that sharp mouth curl in a will-nothing-teach-the-old-fuddy-duddy expression.

He had been wrong last time. This time he knew he couldn't be. No one would have known of his folly if he hadn't alerted Howard before he had proof. It wouldn't matter if he failed this time, for no one would know except himself. They would think he had gone off on some sightseeing tour of his own, to Smithfield or Billingsgate perhaps, taking Baker's advice.

He could be what retired policemen sometimes become, a private detective. That thought had a bitter taste about it and he put it from him. Not retired, not old, but free to pursue a line of his own, bound to no one. No driver to take him, no sergeant to accompany him, no chief to refer back to. And he wasn't going to withhold vital information for long, for, if he had got nowhere by tonight, he would just tell Howard and leave it at that.

It was just eleven-thirty. The rain fell steadily. Obviously, it was going to be one of those days when the rain never lets up. He had left his umbrella in Theresa Street. With unusual extravagance he bought a new one and then he walked jauntily, like a young man, towards Elm Green tube station.

19

*But if the inhabitants . . . will not dwell with them
to be ordered by their laws, then they drive them out
of those bounds which they have limited and
appointed out for themselves.*

IT was a bit like Kenbourne Vale, the district of South
London that was neither Camberwell nor Kennington but a
dismal area lying between them called Wilman Park. The
resemblance lay in the slummy greyness of the place, the
absence of trees, rather than in the houses, for those in Wilman Park were small and tightly packed in streets standing
at true right angles to each other. Wexford supposed that the
third temple of the Children of the Revelation was probably
situated in a similar district of some industrial city in the
north of England. Strange sects do not abound among the rich
who have their heaven here and need not rely on future bliss.

He found Artois Road which bisected Wilman Park and
walked briskly along it between the puddles, passing women
coming back from the shops before they shut for early clos-
ing. They were mothers and daughters mostly, with the
daughter's children shielded from the rain in hooded prams.
He recognised it as the working-class pattern, mother and
daughter going everywhere together, shopping together, not
divided by the girl's marriage. Somewhere here there might be
a mother who walked alone because her daughter had been
divided from her. Or were the Children excluded from such

patterns, as they seemed to be excluded from everything, making their own customs and denying society?

The temple was so small and the rain so torrential that he almost went by without seeing it. He retraced his steps and contemplated it, glad of his umbrella. It was recognisable as the sister, if not the twin, of the one in Garmisch Terrace. The circle of red glass was smaller, the gable shallower, the garden-shed door painted a sticky green, but an identical plaque, signifying the nature of the place, had been cemented into the brickwork which in this case was a plain dull red. The shrubs, against which Loveday had posed, were now a leafless tangle, dripping water on to the pavement.

As in Garmisch Terrace, the temple was the connecting link between two rows of houses, squat mean houses here of yellow brick with stone bays. In one of its immediate neighbours Morgan had been a lodger. In which? Newspapers give the names of streets where defendants and witnesses live, not their house numbers. But it wasn't difficult to guess. One of the houses had daffodils coming into bud in a window box, a television aerial on its roof, red and yellow curtains; the other squatted, its windows blanked out with dark green blinds, behind a tiny front garden whose soil was hidden beneath a layer of concrete.

One of the blinds lifted an inch when he banged on the door —there was no bell, no knocker, only a letter box—but it fell again instantly. The activities of private detectives are limited. They cannot demand entrance or get warrants. He knocked again, and this time there was no movement at the window. He could hear nothing from inside the house, but he sensed hostility as if the people within were ill-wishing him. Strange. Even if they had something to hide, they couldn't know who he was. He might be the gasman, he might be delivering something. A voice behind him made him turn round. A postman with parcels coming out of a red van.

'You won't get in there, mate. They never let no one in.'

'Why not, for God's sake?'

'That's it,' said the postman, grinning. 'For God's sake.

155

They're too religious, see, to talk to the likes of you or me. They call themselves Children of the Revelation. A lot of them live around here, and they won't none of them let no one into their houses.'

'What, not even open their doors?'

'Some do that,' the postman admitted, 'but you can't get inside.'

'Can you tell me where the others live?'

'One lot at 56 and another lot at 92. The 56 lot, they'll *speak* to you, I'll give them that.'

So the refusal to admit him on the part of the occupants of the house next to the temple held no particularly sinister implication. He went to number 56, another grim little house with weeds instead of concrete in its front garden, and the door was answered rather reluctantly by an elderly man in a shiny black suit.

'I'm sorry. I know it's raining, but I can't let you in. What do you want?' His was a flat, cold voice, almost mechanical. Words were necessary for the business of living, Wexford thought, not to grace life, not to be chosen with care for smoothing the path, expressing feelings, pleasing the listener. He remembered what Teal had said.

'I'm writing a book on Christian sects,' he lied unblushingly. 'I wondered if you could give me . . . ?'

In the same dull monotone the man reeled off a list of dates, named the three temples and told Wexford that there were five hundred of the elect on the face of the earth.

'And your Shepherd?' Wexford interrupted him.

'He has a room in the house next to the temple, but they won't open the door to you there.' He gave a sigh as of one who had striven in vain against the temptations of the world. 'They have kept to a purer and straighter way then I. I married *out*.'

'How about number 92?' Wexford began. He got no further for the door was firmly closed in his face. There was nothing for it but to go to Ivy Street, and if that failed, begin a house-to-house in search of the 'brides'.

He had a sandwich in a pub and, feeling almost as guilty as a Child of the Revelation who had opened the door to one of God's rejects, a pint of bitter. Then he phoned Dora to stop her worrying, telling her he was off on a tour with Dearborn and didn't know when he would be home. The rain had slackened slightly. He asked the barman the way to Ivy Street and set off into the back doubles of Artois Road.

The house was a little detached villa with gnomes and an overflowing birdbath in its front garden. It looked shut up. No one answered when he rang the bell and he turned away to come face to face once more with the helpful postman.

'Mrs Morgan's away. Her married daughter's ill and she's gone to look after the son-in-law. Half a tick, while I take this parcel next door.'

Having decided to pump him, Wexford waited impatiently for the postman to return. What he called 'half a tick' became ten minutes' chat with the recipient of the parcel, but at last he came back, whistling cheerfully.

'What about the other daughter?'

'Got a day off from work. I saw her go out half an hour back.'

'I see.' Another disappointment, if you could call finding someone's daughter alive instead of dead a disappointment. 'Did you know Morgan?'

'Not to say know,' said the postman. 'I know *of* him. I used to see him about.'

'Did you ever see him about with a girl?'

The postman laughed. He didn't seem to want to know who Wexford was or why he was asking. 'Morgan was a dark horse,' he said. 'Most of Revelationers didn't know what he was up to till it all came out. Except the girls, that is. One or two of them called themselves Mrs Morgan, had letters addressed to them as Mrs Morgan, as bold as brass.'

'Can you remember which ones?'

'I remember Hannah Peters all right. She was the one as he went through a form of marriage with. That's how his little games came to light. Young Hannah got a letter addressed to

157

Mrs Morgan, her dad got suspicious and then the bomb went up. A lot of other women started complaining. Mind you, his wife had chucked him out years ago but they're not divorced. She says she'll never divorce him. A very vindictive woman is Mrs Morgan and you can't blame her.'

'Can you tell me where Miss Peters lives?'

'Work on a paper, do you?'

'Something like that,' said Wexford.

'I only ask,' said the postman, 'because it seems hard on a feller your age, especially in this weather. Wear the old ones out first, eh?'

Wexford swallowed his humiliation as best he could and managed an unamused grin. The postman gave him the address. 'I daresay she'll be at work now?' he said.

'Not her. The Revelationers don't let their daughters go to work, but I don't reckon you'll see her. They won't let you in.'

But they might open the door. Hannah herself might do that. What he needed now was a piece of luck, one of those near-miracles that had sometimes come his way in the past, clearing and illuminating the path he must follow. And he thought it had happened when, turning into Stockholm Street, he saw the frizzy-haired girl of the newspaper photograph come out of the corner house where the Peters family lived.

She held a letter in her hand which she thrust into the pocket of her long dark raincoat to protect it from the rain, and she paused on the step, darting quick glances about her. Timidly, she came out into the street. It was only a shabby back street where she had probably lived all her life and but for him it was deserted, but she peered about and hesitated as if she were a schoolgirl, separated from her party and lost in a foreign city. Then she walked rapidly towards a pillar box, her head down, keeping custody of her eyes like a nun.

Wexford followed her, and suddenly he felt shy himself. He had an idea, although it was without foundation, that the letter was for Morgan. She started violently when he spoke to her, gasped and put her hand up to cover her mouth.

'Miss Peters, I'm a policeman. I'm only talking to you in

the street because I was afraid I wouldn't be admitted to your home.'

Where did they go to school, these girls? Or did the Revelationers run special schools for their children? Did they never meet outsiders? He wondered if he was the first outsider she had spoken to since she had passed through the terror of the court, an experience which must have been torture to her, enough to shake her reason. Spoken? Was she going to speak now?

She had a plain, unformed face, half-covered still by her hand. No make-up, no rings on her hand. Her body was flat under the stiff heavy coat.

'Miss Peters . . .' Rapidly and rather awkwardly, for she gave him no help, he told her what he wanted and why he was there, accosting her in the rain. He didn't think she was frightened of him, but perhaps she was frightened of God. She scanned the street, her hand now a fist tapping her chin, but before she spoke to him she looked down at her feet. She wouldn't meet his eyes.

'Father would turn me out if he saw me. He was going to turn me out after . . . after . . . Mother made him let me stay.'

The strangest thing in all this strangeness, Wexford thought, was that she should have wanted to stay. But perhaps it wasn't so strange. Hatch out a wild bird, rear it in a cage, and when you set it free it will perish or be destroyed by its fellows. Easing his umbrella over her so that they were both sheltered by it, he began talking to her soothingly, apologising, explaining how important it was for him to know. But all the time he was thinking of the word which lay outside her experience, of the girls like Louise Sampson and Verity Bate who snapped their fingers at their parents, who lived where they liked and with whom they liked, to whom a tyrannical father, wielding real power, was a fictional monster they read about in books written in the distant past. It was almost unbelievable that such opposites as they and Hannah Peters could co-exist in the same city and the same century.

Without looking up, she said, 'I never heard of a girl called Loveday.' She shivered. 'She didn't have to go to the court. What was her real name?'

Wexford shook his head, feeling paralysed by her dull slow voice, her ox-like acceptance of oppression.

'Perhaps she left your congregation in the past twelve months?'

'Mary went away to be a teacher, and Sarah went and Rachel. Edna married out. They all went away.' She didn't speak wistfully but as of some dire enormity. 'My father will punish me if I don't go home now.'

'Their addresses?' he pleaded.

'Oh, no. No, no. Mary was at the court.' It cost her something to say that, he thought. Mary too, had been one of Morgan's brides. She struggled with an emotion no one had ever taught her existed or could be controlled. There were tears on her face or perhaps just rain. 'You must go to the Shepherd,' she said, and ducked out from under the umbrella.

'They won't let me into the house!'

She called back to him something about a prayer meeting that night. Then she ran home through the rain, the caged creature escaping from predators and the humane that would set it free. Back to the cage, the safety of a living death.

Wexford had been shaken by the interview. Hannah Peters bore no physical resemblance to Loveday Morgan, and yet he felt that it was to the latter he had been talking. Here, alive and in a different skin, was the dead girl, the shy, frightened, badly-dressed girl who didn't know how to make friends and was scarcely fit to be employed. At last she had been revealed to him, the cemetery walker, the Bible reader. Teal had known her and had seen her rare, wondering smile; Lamont had sat with her, witness her tortured silences; with a shrug, Dearborn had dismissed her ugly gaucheness. And now he too had seen her, or seen perhaps her ghost.

The street was empty again, the ghost gone. But she had left him a message. He must take the only way open to him now of catching her people outside their prisons.

20

In dim and doubtful light they be gathered together,
and more earnestly fixed on religion and devotion.

DARKNESS came early after that day of torrents. Sitting
in a lorry driver's retreat, his raincoat steaming in the
red glow of an electric fire, Wexford watched the fluorescent
lamps come on in Artois Road. The wet pavements threw back
scarlet and blue and orange reflections of neon overhead. The
sky was red and vaporous, any stars which might have been
up there quenched by the glare. He wondered when the
prayer meeting would begin. Surely not before seven? Hungry
in spite of tea and a doughnut, he ordered a labourer's meal,
a forbidden sinful meal of sausages and chips and fried eggs.

According to Crocker and Dora and their gloomy disciples,
he ought to have been dead by now, for he had broken all
their rules. He had worked when he should have rested, eaten
saturated fats when he should have fasted, gone out at night,
worried and today forgotten all about his pills. Why not break
one more and he hanged for a sheep?

The ultimate forbidden fruit would be to go back into that
pub he had visited at lunchtime and drink spirits. He found it
and had a double Scotch. Far from laying him out, it filled
him with well-being, and he made up his mind then and there
to defy them all. No one but a fool follows a regimen that
debilitates him while moderate indulgence makes him feel
good.

While he had been drinking the rain had stopped. He sniffed

the smell of London after rain, smoky, gaseous, with here and there other scents infiltrating, the odour of frying food and stranger oriental platters, the whiff of a French cigarette. They faded as he walked into the residential depths of Artois Road where the blue-white lamps looked too smart for this hinterland. Another light glowed ahead of him, a round red light like a Cyclops eye, and he saw that he was too late. The prayer meeting had begun. He stood outside the temple and heard the voices of the Children, intoning together sometimes, then one single voice raised in spontaneous praise or perhaps commination. How many hours before they came out? And would they talk to him when they did?

The house where the Shepherd lodged, where Morgan had lodged, looked entirely deserted now, no slits of lights showing at the edges of the blinds. The concrete garden lay under a sheet of water which was black because it had no light to mirror. There were perhaps fifty houses like this one in Wilman Park, vaults for the living. Rachel and Mary and Sarah had gone away . . . He hoped that now they wore scent and false eyelashes and feathers and flowers and sat on steps with their boy friends eating crisps out of paper bags.

Morgan must have met his brides somewhere and not under this severe roof. Did he walk with them, sneak off for clandestine love in the *temple*? Wexford wrinkled his nose in distaste. If he had some neighbour would surely have seen him, perhaps even seen him promenading with the chosen one of the moment.

The house next door showed plenty of light and the curtains weren't even drawn. He rang a bell that chimed, but when she came to admit him his heart sank. She smiled enquiringly. Her eyes were blue and vacant and she supported herself on a white stick.

She was a very old woman, not far off eighty, and she had just enough sight left, he guessed, to make out the shape of him on her doorstep. He didn't want to alarm her, so he explained who he was and why he was there before beginning to retreat. She was no use to him, although he couldn't put it so bluntly. Her blindness disqualified her.

'I was just going to make a cup of tea,' she said. 'Would you like one? My husband was in the force. You'll have heard of him. Wally Lyle.'

Wexford shook his head, then remembered she couldn't see. 'I'm a stranger in these parts,' he said. 'I won't keep you, Mrs Lyle. Perhaps you could just tell me the name of the people next door?'

'Vickers,' she said, and she chuckled. 'You won't get inside there. The only person she ever lets in is the electric meter man. They haven't got no gas.' Her cheerfulness moved him. Here she was, alone, blind, very old, but she could still joke, still find some zest in living. When she said, 'You may as well have that tea. I know how it is on the beat all day,' he agreed on an impulse. She couldn't see that he wasn't in uniform. She wanted a chat about her husband and old times. Why not? He had to pass the time somehow until the temple disgorged its throng.

All the lights were on in the hall and the little rooms. Light must help her, he decided, watching her edge her way to the brighter lamp of the kitchen like a moth. But it was he who finally made the tea and carried their two cups into the front room. All the while she kept close beside him, and when he went to sit by the window, waiting for the temple door to open and send a shaft of light out on to the pavement, she came and sat next to him, hooking her stick over the arm of her chair.

The little pokey living room was crammed with furniture, loaded down with ornaments. He wondered that she could move among all this bric-à-brac without hurting herself or knocking things over, and he recalled his own clumsiness in Howard's house. While she told him anecdotes of her husband's career, he observed the dexterity with which she handled her teacup, and he marvelled.

'How long have you lived here, Mrs Lyle?' he asked gently.

'Forty years. Them Vickerses were here before we come.'

163

'They're quite an elderly couple, then?'

'Not this lot. His mum and dad. I call this one *young* Vickers.' She peered into Wexford's face. 'I daresay he'd be old to you—about fifty he is, but a chip off the old block.'

'And you've never been into their house?'

She liked to talk about the dead Wally Lyle and she returned to him. 'My husband tried to get in there once, years and years ago. Young Vickers and his sister were schoolkids then, and the school sent round this doctor on account of Rebecca—that was the sister—having scarlet fever. They wouldn't have no doctor, you see. Revelationers don't believe in doctors, let their kids die rather than have the doctor.'

'So your husband was called in on account of being a policeman?' Wexford was interested in spite of the irrelevance of all this. 'Did he make them admit the doctor?'

Mrs Lyle laughed shrilly. 'Not likely. He banged and banged in the door till old Vickers come out, and old Vickers cursed him. It made your blood run cold to hear it. My husband said he'd never have nothing to do with them again and he never did.'

'And that was the only contact you ever had with them?'

She looked a little sheepish. 'The only contact *he* did. I never let on to him how I helped Rebecca run away and get married. He'd have given it to me hot and strong, being as he was in the force.'

Rebecca, a girl who had run away . . .

He spoke rather sharply. 'When was that, Mrs Lyle?'

She dashed his faint hope. 'Must be thirty years. It's her brother as lives there now. He got married and had kids and they've all gone now too. God knows where.'

She sighed and fell silent. Wexford watched the dark pavement, growing impatient. Mrs Lyle finished her tea and set the cup down correctly in its saucer. Her blue, filmed eyes were turned on his face now and he sensed that she wanted to make some sort of confession to him.

'What I did,' she said, and her expression was sly, almost naughty, 'I often thought maybe it was against the law, but I never dared ask my husband, never breathed a word about it.'

'What did you do?' Wexford put laughter and encouragement into his voice, for it was no use showing them on his face.

'Won't do no harm telling you after all these years.' She grinned, enjoying herself. 'Rebecca wanted to get married to a fellow she'd met, fellow called Foster who wasn't one of *them*, and her dad he put his foot down and they shut her up in there. Just a prisoner she was, shut up in her bedroom. She used to write notes and throw them to me out of the window. I could see to read in them days. I was all for putting a spoke in the wheel of them Revelationers and I had young Foster in here, jollying him along, and one day when they was all in church we got a ladder and stuck it up at the window and down she come. Like a play it was.'

The orchard walls are high and hard to climb and the place death, considering who thou art, if any of my kinsmen find thee here . . . 'It must have been,' he said.

'I often have a good laugh about it to this day. Mind you, it'd have been better if I'd ever found out what they thought about it but I never did. I'd like to have seen old Vickers' face when he knew the bird had flown. Rebecca got married and she wrote to me, telling me bits of news, but that's stopped now. No good getting letters when you can't read them and you've no one to read them to you, is it?' Mrs Lyle laughed merrily at the doleful situation she had described. 'Vickers—the son, that is—he got married and they had kids but they've all gone off one by one. Couldn't stand it at home. And now there's just the two of them alone in there. Young Vickers—I call him that but he must be all of fifty—he never speaks to me. I reckon he knows what I did for Rebecca. I often have a good laugh when I think of her and that ladder and young Foster like a blessed Romeo. A bit of luck for her that was, catching him. She was nothing to look at and she had a great big mole on the side of her nose . . .'

The temple door must have opened, for a pale stream of

165

light seeped out across the wet stones and people began to appear on the pavement. Wexford, who had been waiting for this to happen, ignored it and turned to face Mrs Lyle, although he knew she couldn't see him.

'A mole in the side of her nose?'

'Stuck there between her nose and her cheek like.' Mrs Lyle jabbed a finger at her own apple complexion. 'My husband used to say she could have had that seen to, only seeing they didn't believe in doctors . . .'

'Where did she go?'

'South-west Ten her address was. I've got letters about somewhere. You'll have to look for them yourself. But I'll tell you one thing, Rebecca won't get you in that house next door. It'd take one of them bulldozers to do that.'

Wexford stood in the bay window and watched the congregation disperse. The women wore dull fashionless, rather than old-fashioned, coats and hats in black or grey or fawn, the men, even the young men, black suits topped by dark raincoats. Among them, like a crow, moved the Shepherd in his black robe, shaking hands, murmuring farewells until all but two were gone. This pair, evidently a married couple, stood arm-in-arm, waiting for him. Then the three of them filed slowly into the house next door. Briefly Wexford caught a glimpse of them mirrored darkly in the pool of water, three strange people crossing the Styx into their own underworld. The front door shut with a slam.

'You looking at young Vickers?' said Mrs Lyle who had the hypersensitivity of the blind. 'I wish my grandson was here to blow him a raspberry. All the kids round here do that, and good luck to them.'

'Better look for those letters now, Mrs Lyle.'

They went upstairs, the old woman leading the way. She took him into her bedroom which had the jumble sale look of rooms occupied by old people and in which they have grown old. Apart from the usual furniture there were workboxes, wooden and wicker, stacked one on top of the other,

166

trunks under the bed and trunks covered with dust sheets which were themselves piled with old magazines and old albums. Two of those miniature chests of drawers, dear to the hearts of the Victorians, stood on the massive tallboy, and above them on the wall was a what-not, crammed full of letters and papers and little boxes and old pens and jars of hairpins.

'It might be in here,' said Mrs Lyle, 'or it might be in the other rooms.'

Wexford looked into the other rooms. None of them was exactly untidy. Nor were they rooms for people to live in. They were the repositories for the results of sixty years of hoarding, and it was apparent to his practised eye that some crazy filing system had been employed in the days when Mrs Lyle still had her sight.

She seemed to sense that he was taken aback. A note came into her voice that was not quite malice but faintly revengeful. She said, 'You've got a long job.' She meant, 'You can see and I can't, so you get on with it.'

He got on with it, beginning in her bedroom. Perhaps it was the smell of these souvenirs, merely musty to him but evocative to her of the occasions they commemorated, which made her face go strange and dreamy, though not unhappy, her hand shake a little as she touched the cards and photographs he lifted from the drawers. He fetched the old brass bedlamp and put it on the tallboy to give him light, and in its yellow radiance, moted with dust, he explored the archives of Mrs Lyle's long life.

She had been a great correspondent and she had kept every letter, every birthday and Christmas card she had ever received. Some male relative had been a philatelist so she had kept the envelopes too, but the collector had never come for his stamps which had accumulated in their thousands on envelopes and scraps torn from envelopes. The late policeman's love letters were there, bound in ribbon from a wedding cake, pieces of ancient and petrified icing still adhering to it. Every year he had sent her a Valentine. He found five in the tallboy, and then he began on the workboxes, seven more in there.

167

'I never throw anything away,' said Mrs Lyle happily.

He didn't say the cruel thing aloud, but he asked it of himself. Why didn't she? Why did she keep these cards, these cake boxes, these locks of babies' hair, these greetings telegrams and these reams of newspaper cuttings? She was blind; she would never be able to see any of them again. But he knew she kept them for another reason. What matter if she never again read the policeman's writing or looked at his picture and those of her posterity? They were the bricks of her identity, the fabric of the walls which kept it safe and the windows through which, though sightless, it could still look out upon its world. His own identity had been too precariously shaken in recent weeks for him to reproach someone who hoarded and harvested and stored to preserve her own.

And he could see. His eye didn't hurt him at all. Even in this dull and dusty light he could read the spidery writing and distinguish the faces in the cloudy sepia photographs. By now he felt that he could have written Mrs Lyle's biography. It was all here, every day of her life, keeping her alive and a unique personality, waiting to be burned by a grandson when she needed it no longer.

They moved on into the next room. Wexford didn't know what time it was; he was afraid to look at his watch. There must be easier ways of finding Rebecca Foster. If only he could remember where it was that he had seen her for the first time . . .

He wished he had begun in the smallest bedroom, for it was there that he found it. He unstrapped a suitcase, unlocked it, opened it. The case contained only letters, some still in their envelopes, some loose, their sheets scattered and mixed with others. And here it was at last. '36, Biretta St., S.W.10. June 26th, 1954. Dear May, Sorry to hear you are having trouble with your eyes . . .'

'Well, that didn't take too long, did it?' said Mrs Lyle. 'I hope you've put all my things back right, not mixed up. I like to know where they are. If you've done, I'll see you off the premises and then I think I'll get to bed.'

21

*He made the proverb true, which saith: He that
shooteth oft, at last shall hit the mark.*

HIS last day. He didn't think of it as the last day of his
holiday but as his last opportunity to solve this case. And
it was the first time he had really known what it is to be set a
deadline. In the past, of course, at Kingsmarkham, the chief
constable had pressed him and there had sometimes been
threats of calling in the Yard, but no one had ever said, You
have twenty-four hours. After that time has elapsed, the case
will be taken out of your hands. No one was saying it now
except himself.

Howard had ceased to regard him as being involved in it.
Come to that, he had never said, This is your case. Solve it
for me. How could he, in his position? All he had asked for
were his uncle's ideas and his uncle's advice, and with Wexford's failure he had given up asking even that. Not that he
gave any sign of being disappointed, but he pinned his faith
now to Baker and it was of Baker that he had talked the
night before.

Wexford had been too tired to take much of it in, gathering
only that Gregson had been remanded in custody on a charge
of assaulting a police officer. Baker still thought of him as his
prime suspect, but just the same he was pursuing other lines.
The scarf was interesting him at the moment and he was much
concerned about an interview he had had with one of the

tenants of Garmisch Terrace. Wexford couldn't summon up energy to ask questions, and Howard too was tired, his foot paining him, and he let his uncle go off to bed, wishing him good night with the optimistic assurance that the case might well be solved before the Wexfords left on the Saturday.

It might well, Wexford reflected on the morning of his last day, but not by Baker.

The women had long given up waiting at the foot of the stairs for him and with regard to breakfast he took pot luck. He felt perfectly well. Yesterday's exercise had taken off more weight while the meals had added none, and even doubtful solicitous Dora had to admit that his holiday had done its good work. It was hard for him to realise that this Friday was just the last day of their holiday for her, a time for packing and going out to buy last-minute gifts. Her only concern was whether or not she had remembered the order for milk to be left on Saturday, and would their little corner shop keep a loaf of bread for her?

'What did you say?' said her husband.

'The bread, Reg. I said I hoped Dixons would keep me a loaf of bread.'

'You said the corner shop . . .' That was where he had seen her! Not, of course, at Dixons down the road from him in Kingsmarkham, but at a little place that might have been its twin opposite a rose-pink house in Fulham. All those hours wasted, rummaging through the storeplace of a life! 'Pity you didn't mention it before,' he said abruptly.

They looked at him as if he were mad, but Denise often did that. 'How are you going to amuse yourself today, Uncle Reg?'

'I shall be all right.'

'Going to see St Thomas for the last time?'

'*Sir* Thomas.' He smiled at her, liking her scented prettiness, glad that he would soon be away from her speckless housekeeping and her dangerous plants. 'Don't you worry about me. I've got things to do. Howard get off all right?'

'Someone came to drive him.'

He waited until they had left the house to buy toys for his grandchildren, and then he walked down past the back way into St Mark and St John, catching sight of a red head by the gates that probably belonged to Verity Bate. She reminded him of his previous failure. He wouldn't fail again, not this time. Everything was falling beautifully into place. He even knew just why Loveday had picked on Belgrade Road and that colourful house opposite the shop as an address to give Peggy Pope. It was straight there that he was going. Why bother with Biretta Street which lay far off his course in the river-bound peninsula that is Chelsea but looks like Wilman Park or Kenbourne Vale?

The shop was ahead of him now, price reductions scrawled on its window, vegetables outside in boxes, a mongrel dog tied up to a lamp standard. He went inside. The shop was full of people, a long queue of women with long shopping lists. Two assistants were serving, a young girl and a woman with a pink wen pushing her nose slightly askew.

There was nothing for it but to wait until the place emptied, if it ever did on a Friday when shoppers stocked up with weekend provisions. He paced up and down the street, time passing with maddening slowness. Years and years ago, when he was young, he had felt like this, arriving too early for a date with a girl, killing time. The cold mist made him shiver and his fingers felt numb. Pity he hadn't thought of putting gloves on. Gloves . . . In all these enquiries of his he mustn't forget the girl with the gloves.

When he went back for the fourth time to the shop door, all but one of the queue had gone and this last one was being served by the girl. His woman, his longed-for date, had gone to the window and was stacking soap packets in a pyramid.

'Mrs Foster?' he said, his throat dry.

She stepped back, surprised, and nodded. The mole, which might once have marred a pretty face, was now only an ugly feature among general worn ugliness. She looked about fifty. Ah, the orchard walls are high and hard to climb . . .

'I'm a police officer. I should like to talk to you.'

When she spoke he heard the voice of a Child of the Revelation, accentless, dull, economical.

'What about?' she said.

'Your niece,' said Wexford. 'Your brother's daughter.

She didn't argue or expostulate but told the girl to see to the shop and led him into a small room at the rear.

'I've been talking to Mrs Lyle,' he said.

The blood poured into her face and she pressed her ill-kept hands together. It was impossible to imagine her as the young girl, the Juliet, who had climbed down a ladder into her lover's arms. 'Mrs Lyle . . . Does she still live down there? Next door to my brother?'

'She's blind now. She knew nothing, only your address.'

'Blind,' said Mrs Foster. 'Blind. And I'm a widow and Rachel . . .' To his horror she began to cry. She cried as if she were ashamed of her tears, scrubbing them away as they fell. 'The world's all wrong,' she said. 'It ought to be changed.'

'Maybe. Tell me about Rachel.'

'I promised her . . .'

'Your promises mean nothing now, Mrs Foster. Rachel is dead.' He had broken it without preamble but he regretted nothing, for he could tell that her niece had very little to do with her grief. She had been crying for herself, perhaps a little for Mrs Lyle. Who had ever shed a tear for Loveday Morgan?'

'Dead,' she said as she had said 'blind'. 'How, dead?'

He explained and all the time he was speaking her face was stony. 'Now it's your turn,' he said.

'She came to my house in July, last July.' The voice grated on him. It was even, monotonous, without rise or fall. 'My brother turned her out when he found she was expecting. She was small and she didn't eat much and she didn't show till nearly the end. My brother told her to get out.'

He had guessed but he could hardly believe it. In these days? In London in the nineteen seventies? Although she had

172

emancipated herself from her upbringing, Mrs Foster had about her something Victorian, and it was a Victorian situation, chronicled in a thousand novels, that she was describing.

'You can't credit it?' she said. 'You don't know what the Children are. She came to me because there was no one else. She'd never heard of people, societies, that look after girls like her. I'd have thought she was simple if I hadn't been like that myself once.'

'The baby?'

'She hadn't seen a doctor. I told her to go and see one. She wouldn't. She'd never been to a doctor in her life. The Children don't have doctors. She wouldn't go to the Assistance. I kept her. I had this job and two jobs cleaning. What else could I do? One day I got home from work and she'd had the baby all by herself in my bedroom.'

'Without any assistance?'

Mrs. Foster nodded. 'I made her have a doctor then. I sent for my own. He was very angry with me but what could I do? He sent in the midwife every day and I registered the baby in Chelsea, up in the King's Road.'

'Morgan was the father?'

'Yes. She said she was his wife and when he came out of prison they'd be married properly. I knew that wasn't true. He had a wife living. We looked after the baby between us and when she got work, cleaning work, sometimes I'd take it with me or she'd take it with her.'

'And then?'

Mrs Foster hesitated. The girl in the shop called her and she said, 'I'm coming. I'm coming in a minute.' She turned tiredly to Wexford. 'It was adopted. Rachel loved it, but she agreed. She knew it wasn't possible for us to keep it all on our own. We had to work, both of us, and women don't like it if you take a baby with you. But Rachel was no worker, anyway. She wasn't used to it. She was crazy about television. It was new to her, you see. All she wanted was to sit about all day, watching the television with the baby on her lap. She said she'd like to be somewhere where she could watch

173

it all day long. Then the baby went and being in my house without it got her down, so she left and got a room. I never heard from her. I thought maybe my brother had taken her back. All she'd been through hadn't stopped her wanting to be one of the Children . . .' Mrs Foster's voice tailed forlornly away.

'Who adopted the baby? Was it done through a society?'

'I can't tell you that. I promised. Rachel never knew. We thought it best she shouldn't know.'

'I must know.'

'Not through me. I promised.'

'Then I must go to the Children's Department,' said Wexford.

The phone book told him he would find it in Holland Park and he waited for a taxi to take him there. But he knew the answer already, the whole answer, and as he stood at the kerb he began carefully arranging mentally the complete sequence of events from Rachel Vickers' arrival in Biretta Street to her death as Loveday Morgan in Kenbourne Vale cemetery.

Poor Baker. Just for once he was to be cheated of his triumph, forestalled by the old fuddy-duddy from the country. Wexford felt gently amused to think of them all there in Kenbourne, pursuing lines which would lead to dead ends, running off at tangents, clinging obstinately to their need to pin it on a boy van driver. All there at the police station—except Sergeant Clements. And he would be in court, getting his order. Or perhaps, even at this moment, failing to get it?

Howard and Baker were at the Yard. Everyone knew Clements was taking the day off and why he was. Pamela told Wexford she didn't expect the superintendent to put in a further appearance that day.

The snapshot Pamela had found on Howard's desk was no longer there. Someone had taken it or put it away. Instead, Mrs Dearborn's blue scarf lay there, enclosed but not concealed by a case of clear plastic. It had the look of a pre-

174

wrapped Christmas gift but for the neat official label stuck to the side of the case.

Wexford shrugged, thanked Pamela and went out. To get to Elm Green tube station he made a detour through the cemetery. In the gathering fog the winged victory was ghost-like and the black horses, half-veiled in vapour, seemed to plunge on the air itself without support, without anchorage. Beneath them the royal tombs had lost their solidity as had the still trees, spectres of trees rather, floating, rootless and grey. Water drops, condensed mist, clung to the thready brambles. Obelisks, broken columns, angels with swords, a hunter with two dead lions at his feet . . .

'He who asks questions is a fool.
    He who answers them is a greater fool . . .'

Wexford smiled.

22

*The murder being once done, he is in less fear and
more hope that the deed shall not be betrayed or
known, seeing the party is now dead and rid out of
the way, which only might have uttered and disclosed
it.*

A LAST day well spent. Wexford was a poor typist but
he would have been glad of the use of a typewriter
now. He had to write the whole thing out on sheet after sheet
of Basildon Bond, using Dora's old fountain pen. It was
after seven when he finished and then he went downstairs to
wait for Howard.

His plan was to give Howard the report after dinner, and
he envisaged their discussing it quietly in the study, but his
nephew phoned to say he would be delayed and had replaced
the receiver before Wexford had a chance to talk to him.

'You ought to go to bed, dear,' Dora said at ten.

'Why? So that I'll be strong enough to sit in the train? I've
a good mind to stay up all night.'

He opened the book Denise had at last, in despair over his
dilatoriness, fetched him from the library. 'To the Right
Honourable and his Very Singular Good Master, Master
William Cecil Esquire . . . Ralph Robinson wisheth continu-
ance of good health with daily increase of virtue and honour.'
That dedication, with different names substituted, might as well
have served as an introduction to his own report as to Sir

Thomas's masterpiece. He had scarcely read the first paragraph when the phone rang again.

'He wants to talk to you, Uncle Reg. I said you were just off to bed.'

Wexford took the phone in a hand that trembled very slightly. 'Howard?'

Howard's voice was hard, a little disdainful. 'If you're on your way to bed it doesn't matter.'

'I'm not. I was waiting up for you.' Now that the time had come, Wexford found himself strangely reluctant, his voice uncertain. 'There are a few points . . . Well, I've written a sort of report . . . Would you care to . . . ? I mean, my conclusions . . .'

'Could be the same as ours,' Howard finished the sentence for him. 'The scarf? Yes, I thought so. Baker and I have just been to see a friend of yours and what we really need now is a little help from you. If you'll hold the line, I'll put Baker on.'

'Howard, wait. I could come over.'

'What, now? To Kenbourne Vale?'

Wexford decided to be firm, not to argue at all. He saw clearly and coldly that he was failing for the second time, but he wouldn't give in without some sort of fight, not let Baker steal his last faint thunder. 'I'll take a taxi,' he said.

The expected wail came from Dora. 'Oh, darling! At this hour?'

'I said I was going to stay up all night.'

What amazed him was that some of the shops were still open at ten minutes to midnight and people were still buying groceries for strange nocturnal feasts. In the launderettes the bluish-white lights were on and the machines continued to turn. His cab took him through North Kensington where the night people walked, chatting desultorily, strolling, as if it were day. In Kingsmarkham anybody still out would be hastening home to bed. Here the sky wore its red, starless glow, above the floating lights, the sleepless city. They came into Kenbourne Lane. The cemetery was like a pitch-black cloud, only visible because its mass was darker than the sky. Wexford felt the muscles of his chest contract as he realised they were nearly there. Soon he would be facing Baker. If only there might be a chance of Howard reading his report first ...

He had had a foolish feeling that there might be a sort of reception committee awaiting him, but there was no one in the foyer but the officers on duty. And when he tried to treat the place as if it was more familiar with him than he with it, walking casually towards the lift, a sergeant called him back to ask his name and his business.

'Mr Wexford, is it? The superintendent is expecting you, sir.'

That was a little better. His spirits rose higher when he stepped out of the lift and saw Howard standing alone in the corridor outside his office.

'You've been very quick.'

'Howard, I just want to say ...'

'You want to know about Gregson. I guessed you would and I meant to mention it on the phone. Where d'you think he was on the 25th? Doing that housebreaking job, of all things. The girl who phoned him at Mrs Kirby's was Harry Slade's girl friend to tell him the job was on and give him all the gen. Come on in now, and see Baker. Shall I send down for coffee?'

Wexford didn't answer him. He walked into the office, met Baker's eyes and silently drew his report out of his pocket. The handwritten sheets looked very amateurish, very rustic.

Howard said awkwardly, 'We really only wanted some inside information, Reg. A few questions we had to put to you ...'

'It's all in there. It won't take you more than ten minutes to read the lot.'

Wexford knew he was being hypersensitive, but a man would have had to be totally without perception not to see that resigned and indulgent glance which passed between Baker and Howard. He sat down, sliding his arms out of his raincoat and letting it fall over the back of the chair. Then he stared at the uncurtained window, the thick red sky and the black bulk of the bottling plant. While Howard phoned to order coffee, Baker cast his eyes over, rather than read, the report.

It was ten pages long. He got to page five and then he said, 'All this stuff about the girl's background, it's very edifying, no doubt, but hardly . . .' He sought for a word. ' . . . Germane to this inquiry,' he said.

'Let me see.' Howard stood behind Baker, reading rapidly. 'You've put in a lot of work here, Reg. Congratulations. You seem to have reached the same conclusions as we have.'

'Taking all the evidence,' said Wexford, 'they are the only possible conclusions.'

Howard gave him a quick look. 'Yes, well . . . Maybe the best thing would be for you to sum up for us, Michael.'

The sheets of blue paper were growing rather crumpled now. Baker folded them and dropped them rather contemptuously on the desk top. But when he spoke it wasn't contemptuously. He cleared his throat and said in the uneasy tone of a man who is unaccustomed to graciousness, 'I owe you a bit of an apology, Mr Wexford. I shouldn't have said what I did about wild goose chases and red herrings and all that. But it did look like a red herring at first, didn't it?'

Wexford smiled. 'It looked like a needless complication.'

'Not needless at all,' Howard said. 'Without it we should never have traced the ownership of the scarf. Here's our coffee. Put it down there, Sergeant, thank you. Well, Michael?'

'For a time,' Baker began, 'we were completely put off the scent by the confusion between Rachel Vickers and Dearborn's own stepdaughter. We neglected to bear in mind the circumstantial evidence and we did not then, of course, know that his daughter Alexandra was not his own child.'

Wexford stirred his coffee, although it was black and sugarless. 'How do you know now?' he interrupted.

'Mrs Dearborn told us herself tonight. She was very fran⸺ very open. When she realised the importance of the inq⸺ she told us quite freely that Alexandra—named, she be⸺ after her natural father—is a child she and her husb⸺ adopted privately. Two adoption societies had refu⸺

179

sider them on account of their age, and when the opportunity arose just before Christmas for them to take this baby they jumped at it. Dearborn acted very properly. He intended to adopt legally and through the proper channels. As soon as the child was received into his house in late December, he notified the Children's Department and the court of his intention to adopt. Did you want to say something, Mr Wexford?'

'Only that you make it sound very cold. He loves that child passionately.'

'I don't think we should allow our emotions to be involved. Naturally, the whole thing is painful. Let me resume. Mrs Dearborn has never met Rachel Vickers. All she knew about her came from the girl's aunt, her former charwoman, Mrs Foster, and from the guardian *ad litem*.'

'The girl with the gloves,' said Wexford.

Baker took no notice of this. 'The guardian and Mrs Foster knew the girl as Rachel Vickers, never as Loveday Morgan. Until February 14th, Dearborn also only knew the girl by her true name, he had never seen her and supposed everything would be plain sailing. On that day he came home and told his wife that while he had been showing Alexandra some property he intended to buy in Lammas Grove, Rachel Vickers came out of a shop and recognised her child.' Baker paused. 'I must admit I don't quite understand that, a man pointing out houses to a babe in arms, but I daresay it's irrelevant.' He glanced at Wexford and Wexford said nothing. 'According to Mrs Dearborn,' he went on, 'Rachel asked him if she might see Alexandra again and he agreed, though reluctantly, giving her his office phone number. Mrs Dearborn says—and I believe she is speaking the truth—that she knows of no more meetings between Rachel and her husband. s far as she knows, the girl showed no more interest in the d after that.'

. however,' put in Howard, 'have been told early in this hat Rachel had an interview at Notbourne Properties fter February 14th, and I think we can conclude this interview had nothing to do with an application for a job. What are your views, Reg?'

'Dearborn,' said Wexford slowly, 'wanted to keep the child and Rachel, just as intensely, wanted her back. At that interview in his office she told him she would oppose the granting of his order and he took the highly illegal step of offering her five thousand pounds not to oppose it.'

'How can you possibly know that?'

Wexford shrugged. 'Finish reading my report and you'll know how. Without reading it, you can surely see that this is why Dearborn told his wife no more. He's unscrupulous but Mrs Dearborn isn't. She would never have gone along with him in any scheme to *buy* the child. When did they expect to get the order?'

'On March 24th,' said Baker with a certain triumph. 'If you don't know that, Mr Wexford, I don't see how . . . But let me get on with my ideas of what happened next. Rachel agreed to take the money—some money, we can't say how much—and promised to phone Dearborn to fix a date for this transaction. The date she chose was February 25th and she phoned Dearborn from Garmisch Terrace at one fifteen on that day. They met about an hour later in the cemetery.'

'You've identified the scarf as Mrs Dearborn's?'

'Certainly. That's why we went to see her in the first place. She told us she often wears her husband's sheepskin jacket and probably left the scarf in that jacket pocket. Dearborn met the girl as arranged, but when he was about to part with the money, thought how much easier it would be, how much safer he would be, to keep the money and kill the girl. He would never be sure otherwise that she wouldn't oppose the order just the same. So he strangled her with the scarf and put her body in the Montfort tomb.'

'You helped us again there, Reg,' said Howard. 'It was you who pointed out about its being Leap Year. Dearborn forgot that. He supposed that the last Tuesday of the month had gone by and that the tomb wouldn't be visited until *after* March 24th, by which time he would have his order.'

Wexford reached for his report, fingered it hesitantly and then laid it down again. 'He's confessed all this?' he asked. 'You've talked to him and . . . Have you charged him?'

'He's away from home,' said Baker. 'Up in the north somewhere at some architects' conference.'

'We wanted your *opinion*, Reg,' Howard said rather sharply. 'So much of this is conjecture. As you said yourself it's the only possible conclusion, but we thought you might have something more concrete for us.'

'I said that?'

'Well, surely. I understood you to . . . '

Wexford got up abruptly, pushing back his chair so that it almost fell over. He was suddenly frightened, but not of himself, not any more of failure. 'His wife will get in touch with him!'

'Of course she will. Let her. He's due back tomorrow morning.' Howard looked at his watch. 'This morning, rather. Once he knows he's in danger of not getting that order—his wife will tell him that the court will suspend all action until the matter is cleared up—he'll come hotfoot to us. My God, Reg, she doesn't know we suspect him of murder.'

'But he'll know by now he hasn't a hope in hell of remaining as Alexandra's father?' Wexford gripped the back of the chair. He was shivering. 'Will she have told him that?'

'Unless she's a far more phlegmatic woman than I take her to be, yes.'

He tried to stay calm. He knew his face had grown white, for he could feel the skin shrink and tremble. Baker's face was scornful and sour, Howard's entirely bewildered.

'You wanted my advice. It must be that because you don't want my opinion. My advice to you is to phone Dearborn's hotel now, at once.' Wexford sat down and turned his face to the wall.

'He's in his room,' said Baker, replacing the receiver. 'I don't see the need for all this melodrama. The man's in his room, asleep, but they've gone to check and they'll call us back. I suppose Mr Wexford's idea is they'll find a bundle of clothes under the sheets and the bird flown.'

Wexford didn't comment on that. His hands were clasped tightly together, the knuckles whitened by the strong pressure. He didn't relax them but he relaxed his voice, making conversation for the sake of it. 'What happened about Clements?' he asked, attempting to sound casual.

'He got his order,' Howard said. 'Phoned through to tell us. No difficulty at all.'

'I'll send his wife some flowers,' said Wexford. 'Remind me.' He helped himself to more coffee without bothering to ask permission, but his hand was unsteady and he slopped it on to the desk. Howard didn't say a word.

The phone gave the prefatory click that comes a split second before it rings. Before it rang Wexford had jumped and got the shock over. Three hands went out to the receiver, the other men infected by his dread. It was Howard who lifted it, Howard who said, 'I see. Yes. You've got a doctor? The local police?' He covered the mouthpiece with his hand. His thin face had grown very pale. 'There's a doctor staying in the hotel,' he said. 'He's with Dearborn now.'

'He tried to kill himself,' said Wexford and he said it not as a question but as a statement of fact.

'They think he's dead. They don't know. Some sort of overdose, it sounds like.'

Baker said, attempting a suitable dolefulness, 'Maybe it's the best thing. Horrible, of course, but when you think of the alternative, years inside. In his position I'd take the same way out.'

Howard was talking again, asking sharp questions into the phone. 'What position?' said Wexford. 'You don't still think he did it, do you?'

23

If by none of these means the matter go forward as they would have it, then they procure occasions of debate.

WEXFORD had seen many a dawn in Kingsmarkham, but never till now a London dawn. He parted the curtains at Howard's window and watched the indigo sky split and shred to show between the heavy clouds streaks of greenish light. A little wind, too slight to set the cemetery trees in motion, fluttered a flag on the roof of a distant building. Pigeons had began to coo, to take wing and wheel lazily against the façades of tower blocks which they, foolish creatures and slow to learn, still took for the cliffs of southern Italy from where the Romans had brought them two thousand years before. The roar of the traffic, half-silenced during the small dead hours, was rising again to its full daytime volume.

Apart from himself, the office was empty. As the great red ball of a sun began to rise, thrusting through reddish-black vapourish folds, the street lamps of Kenbourne Vale went out gradually. Wexford went across the room and snapped off the light switch. But no sooner had he found himself in the welcome, restful semi-darkness than the light came on again and Howard limped into the office with Melanie Dearborn.

Her face was haggard, the eye sockets purple with fatigue ¹ fear. She wore trousers and a sweater and over them her ²nd's sheepskin coat. But for all her pain and her anxiety, she hadn't forgotten her manners. Blinking a little against the light, she came up to Wexford and held out her hand. 'I'm so sorry,' she began, 'that we should meet again like this, that these terrible things . . .'

He shook his head, fetched a chair and helped her into it. Then he met Howard's eyes and Howard gave a tiny, almost imperceptible nod, pursing his lips.

'Your husband . . . ?'

'Is going to recover,' Howard answered for her. 'He's in hospital and he's very tired but he's conscious. He'll be all right.'

'Thank God,' Wexford said sincerely.

She looked up at him and managed a weak watery smile. 'Why was I so stupid as to phone him last night? I got in a panic, you see. I couldn't bear to think of him coming home and perhaps finding Alexandra gone. He told me all he'd done to keep her.'

Wexford sat down and drew his chair close to hers.

'What did he do, Mrs Dearborn?'

'I'm afraid to tell you,' she whispered. 'Because if it comes out . . . they may . . . I mean, they could take Alexandra away and not let us . . .'

Wexford looked at Howard, but Howard didn't move a muscle. 'It will be better to tell us,' he said. 'It's always better to tell the truth. And if the bribe wasn't taken . . .'

There was a discouraging cough from Howard and Melanie Dearborn gave a heavy sigh. She snuggled more deeply inside the coat as if, because it was her husband's and he had worn it, she had near to her a comforting part of himself. 'The bribe was offered,' she said.

'How much?' Howard asked gently but succinctly.

'Five thousand pounds.'

Wexford nodded. 'She was to promise not to oppose the order in exchange for that?'

'She did promise. When she came to my husband's office. Then and there they made an appointment to meet in Kenbourne Vale cemetery on February 25th at two-fifteen.'

185

'Why did she change her mind?'

'She didn't exactly. According to Stephen, she was a very simple sort of girl. When he and she met that day she began to talk about how she was going to use the money and give it to someone to look after Alexandra while she was out at work. She didn't even have the sense to realise what she was saying. Stephen said, "But you won't have Alexandra. I'm giving you the money so that I can keep her." And then she put her hand over her mouth—you can imagine—and said, "Oh, Mr Dearborn, but I must keep her. She's all I've got in the world and you won't miss the money." She just didn't *see*.'

Wexford nodded but he said nothing. He had seen the girl, or her ghost, her counterpart, her *doppel-gänger*. Both had been brought up in a strict morality, but a morality which leaves out what ordinary human beings call ethics.

'Stephen was—well, appalled,' Mrs Dearborn went on. 'He said he'd give her more, anything she asked. He was prepared to go up to—oh, I don't know—fifty thousand, I expect. But she couldn't imagine that amount of money.'

'He didn't give her anything?'

'Of course he didn't. She was chattering on about how she'd give a thousand to someone to look after Alexandra and keep the four for the future, and he saw it wasn't any good and he just turned away and left her. He was very quiet and moody that night—I thought it was because he was tired of the way I fretted about Louise. By the middle of the next week he was on top of the world again. I know why that was now. He'd realised who the murdered girl was.'

Howard had listened to it all without intervening, but now he said in a steady cool voice, 'If you're going up to see your husband, Mrs Dearborn, we'd better see about transport for you.'

'Thank you. I'm afraid I'm giving everyone a great deal of trouble.' Melanie Dearborn hesitated and then said in a rush, 'What am I to say to him about—about Alexandra?'

'That depends on the outcome of this case and upon the ~t.'

'But we love her,' she pleaded. 'We can give her a good home. Stephen—he tried to *kill* himself. The bribe wasn't accepted. In the girl's mind it wasn't a bribe at all but a gift, just like the clothes we gave her aunt.'

'Well?' said Wexford to Howard after she had left them, casting over her shoulder a last imploring look.

'The court might, I suppose, see it in that light. But when the evidence given in Dearborn's prosecution . . .'

'What are you going to prosecute him for, Howard? Making a present of money to a poverty-stricken girl, his former servant's niece, so that she could raise a child he was fond of decently? And then withdrawing the offer because the chosen guardians weren't suitable in his eyes?'

'It wasn't like that, Reg, you're being Jesuitical. Dearborn killed her. The scarf was his wife's, in the pocket of that coat which they both wear. He had abundant motive which no one else had. And he had the special knowledge. He put her in a tomb he knew wouldn't be visited until after he had got his adoption order.'

'Knew?' said Wexford. 'He wouldn't have forgotten it was Leap Year. February 29th was his birthday.'

'I don't understand you, Mr Wexford,' said Baker who had just come in and had overheard his last words. 'According to your report you go along with our views entirely.'

'How do you know? You didn't bother to read to the end.'

Howard looked at his uncle, half-smiling as if he understood that this was triumph, this was the end he had asked for and more than Wexford had hoped to attain. He picked up the last two sheets of blue paper and, beckoning Baker to him, read them swiftly. 'We shouldn't be here,' he said when he had finished. 'We should be in Garmisch Terrace.'

'You should,' Wexford retorted. He looked at his watch and yawned. 'I've a train to catch at ten.'

Baker took a step towards him. He didn't hold out this han or attempt to retract anything or even smile. He said, 'I do know how Mr Fortune feels, but I'd take it as a per

187

favour if you'd come with us.' And Wexford understood that this was a frank and full apology.

'There are other trains,' he said, and he put on his coat.

Early morning in Garmisch Terrace, a thin pale sunlight baring the houses in all their dilapidation. Someone had scrawled 'God is dead' on the temple wall, and the Shepherd was in the act of erasing it with a scrubbing brush and a bucket of water. Outside number 22, Peggy Pope, her hair tied up in a scarf, was loading small articles of furniture into a van.

'Going somewhere?' said Wexford.

She shrugged. 'Next week,' she said. 'I thought I owed it to the landlords to give them a week's notice.' Her face, unwashed, unpainted, rather greasy, had a curious spiritual beauty like a young saint's. 'I'm just getting shot of a few of my things.'

Wexford glanced at the driver. It was the Indian tenant. 'Off with him, are you?'

'I'm off *alone*, me and the kid, that is. He's just letting me have a loan of his van. I'm going home to my mother. Nowhere else *to* go, is there?' She thrust a battered record player into the van, wiped her hands on her jeans and went down the area steps. The three policemen followed her.

The stacks of old books were still there, the cumbersome shabby furniture. On the wall a little more paint had peeled away, enlarging the map of that unearthly, Utopian continent. Lamont was in bed, the baby lying restlessly in the crook of his arm.

Peggy showed none of the outraged propriety that might have been evinced by a respectable housewife under these circumstances. She wasn't a respectable housewife but a wandering girl about to leave her lover. Remembering perhaps how Wexford had once before assisted her in moving heavy objects, she seemed to take his presence as a sign that it was in this role that he had reappeared, and she thrust into his arms a opping basket full of kitchen utensils. Wexford shook his at her. He went over to the bed and stared at Lamont

188

who responded first by burying his head in the pillow, then by pulling himself slowly and despairingly into a sitting position.

Howard and Baker came closer to the bed, Peggy watched them. She knew now that something was wrong, that they were not merely here to ask questions. But she said nothing. She was leaving Garmisch Terrace and everything it contained, and perhaps she didn't care.

'Get up, Lamont,' said Baker. 'Get up and get dressed.'

Lamont didn't speak to him. Under the dirty sheet he was naked. His eyes had a naked empty look in them, expressing a total failure, an utter poverty, a lack of love, of possessions, of imagination. Thou art the thing itself, Wexford thought, unaccommodated man is no more than such a poor, bare animal as thou art . . . 'Come along, you know why we are here.'

'I never had the money,' Lamont whispered. He let the sheet drop, took the child in his arms and handed her to Peggy. It was the final renunciation. 'You'll have to look after her now,' he said. 'Just you. I did it for you and her. Would you have stayed if I'd got the money?'

'I don't know,' Peggy said, crying. 'I don't know.'

'I wish,' said Howard tiredly, 'I felt as well as you look. They say a change is as good as a rest, and you haven't had either, but you look fine.'

'I feel fine.' Wexford thought but he didn't say aloud, I'll be glad to get home just the same. 'It's good to be able to read again without feeling you're going to go blind.'

'Which reminds me,' said Howard, 'I've got something for you to read in the train. A parting gift. Pamela went out to the West-End and got it.'

A very handsome copy of *Utopia*, bound in amber calf, tooled in gold. 'So I've got it at last. Thanks very much. If we're going back to Chelsea now, d'you think we could make a detour for me to say good-bye to him?'

'Why not? And in the car, Reg, maybe you'll just clear up a few points for me.'

It was going to be a lovely day, the first really fine day of Wexford's holiday now that his holiday was over. He asked Howard to wind down the window so that he could feel the soft air on his face. 'After I made that first blunder,' he said, 'I realised Dearborn wouldn't have desecrated his cemetery, and then I remembered he'd told me February 29th was his birthday. A man doesn't forget when his own birthday is going to occur, especially when it only really occurs once in every four years. Lamont put her in the Montfort vault because it was outside it that he encountered her—and killed her.'

'What put you on to him in the first place?'

'The way Loveday—I think of her as Loveday, perhaps because she was trying to get out of her darkness into a kind of light—the way she went down to talk to him and wanted to *entrust* something to him. She had nothing to entrust but Alexandra. She approached him and not Peggy partly because she was afraid of Peggy and partly because it was Lamont who mostly cared for his own child.' They entered Hyde Park, a sea of precocious daffodils. Ten thousand saw I at a glance . . . 'She told him she was going to get five thousand pounds, and she must have convinced him in spite of the unlikelihood of it, for he consulted estate agents. I saw a specification he had there for a house costing just under five thousand.'

'She was only going to give him one thousand.'

'I know. I don't suppose he thought of resorting to violence then, but he meant to con the rest out of her.'

'So she phoned Dearborn,' said Howard as they drove past the museums, thronged with tourists this Saturday morning. 'She phoned him at one-fifteen on February 25th to make the appointment.'

'They'd already made it in his office. It was Lamont she phoned. He was in the Grand Duke and he always took his phone calls there. She told him the money was going to be handed over to her in the cemetery that afternoon. He must have waited for her and seen her part from Dearborn, concluding, of course, that she had got the money.'

'Then he waylaid her,' said Howard. 'He asked for his

thousand to start with, but she wouldn't give him even that. She had nothing to give.'

Wexford nodded. 'He desperately wanted to keep Peggy and his child. Nothing was to get in his way now. He strangled her with her own scarf.'

'No, Reg, I can't have that. It was Mrs. Dearborn's scarf.'

'It was once,' said Wexford. 'Dearborn gave it to Loveday's aunt.'

The river was rippling brown and gold, a big brother, dirtier and wider and stronger, of the Kingsbrook. Tonight, Wexford thought, when we've unpacked our bags and the grandchildren have been to get their presents, tonight I'll go down and look at my own river. He got out of the car and walked up to Sir Thomas. This morning the gold cap and the gold chain were almost too dazzling to look at.

Wexford turned to Howard who had limped after him. He tapped his pocket where the new book was. 'More than four hundred years since he wrote that,' he said, 'but I don't know that things have changed all that much for the better, not the way he must have hoped they would. It's a good job he doesn't know. He'd get up off that seat of his and go back to the Tower.'

'Aren't you going to read your new book?' asked Dora when they were in the train, and the outer suburbs, grey streets, red housing estates, white tower blocks, trees like numberless puffs of smoke in the gold mist, flowed past the window.

'In a minute,' said Wexford. 'What have you got there, more presents?'

'I nearly forgot. These two came for you this morning.'

Two parcels, a thick one and a thin one. Who could be sending him parcels? The handwriting on the brown paper wrappings meant nothing. He undid the string in the thin one and a copy of *Utopia* fell out, a paperback version, with a card enclosed, depicting a rabbit in rustic surroundings, and signed with love from Denise's sister-in-law. Wexford snorted.

'Are you all right, darling?' said anxious Dora.

'Of course I'm all right,' Wexford growled. 'Don't start that again.'

The other parcel also contained a book. He wasn't at all surprised to come upon another *Utopia*, second-hand this time but well preserved. The card had a violet border, the name on it printed in gold. 'You forgot this', Wexford read. 'Something to read in the train. You can keep it. One doesn't meet human policemen every day. I.M.T.'

Something to read in the train . . . Tiredness hit him like a physical blow, but he struggled to keep awake, clasping his three new books, staring out of the window. The green country was beginning now, fingers of it groping and inserting themselves into wedges of brick. Soon they would be travelling into the haunch of England, into the swelling downs. Now for *Utopia*, now at last.

Dora bent down and silently picked up the books from the carriage floor. Her husband was asleep.